The Tutor

"Well, Susan," her teacher said, "You certainly didn't do well on your test. Would you be interested in working with a tutor?"

"Well. . . ." Susan stalled for an answer. She wasn't exactly thrilled at the prospect of going over algebra equations with a nerd.

Just then the door opened and Susan turned her head, her silky ponytail swinging. She stopped herself just in time from gasping out loud. This guy couldn't be her tutor. He was by far the cutest boy she'd ever seen.

Books from Scholastic
in the **Couples** series:

TEACHER'S PET

M.E. Cooper

SCHOLASTIC INC.
New York Toronto London Auckland Sydney

ISBN 0-590-40426-1

12 11 10 9 8 7 6 5 4 3 2 1   7 8 9/8 0 1 2/9

Printed in the U. S. A.   01

First Scholastic printing, April 1987

TEACHER'S PET

Chapter
1

"Okay, class," Miss Taylor said in a crisp, efficient voice. "Here are your tests. Nearly all of you did very well." She walked slowly up and down the classroom aisles, handing back each student's paper.

Susan Atkinson watched her algebra teacher get closer to her desk and braced herself. Algebra had never been her best subject, but then again nothing really was. Usually she was happy if she got all B's on her report card, but lately her grades had been slipping even lower.

"Here, Susan." Miss Taylor held out her test as if it were a dead bug. She scowled down at her blonde, blue-eyed student.

It wasn't hard to tell from the expression on Miss Taylor's face that she wasn't exactly pleased. Susan took the test, inhaled deeply for courage, and turned the paper over to see her grade.

She had figured she'd made a C at best. Maybe

a C-minus. But she wasn't ready for that F blazed in red pencil at the top of the page. Even worse was the *Please see me after class* Miss Taylor had scrawled next to the F.

Susan suddenly wished she hadn't eaten that yogurt for lunch — she felt distinctly queasy. She sighed and reached back to twist the end of her pony tail. What was her mother going to say when she found out? Her family had enough problems these days because of her parents' divorce. If she failed a class, it would only add to her mother's worries and that was the last thing Susan wanted to do. And if her *father* learned about the F. . . ! She could hardly stand even *thinking* about it.

Even now, sitting there in algebra, Susan felt a sad, lonely ache as she remembered the afternoon two months before when her father had walked out the front door, suitcase in hand, to move to an apartment in D.C. Sure, he'd promised to see Susan and her sister Amy as much as he could, and he'd kept his word. After all, D.C. wasn't that far from Rose Hill. But nothing was quite the same since he'd left, or since last week, when Susan, her mother, and Amy had moved from their old neighborhood to a smaller house. With so many changes, Susan guessed she'd been too distracted to study much lately. Distracted wasn't even the word for it. It was like having not only a comforting rug pulled out from under her feet but the whole floor, too. Susan shook her head. She couldn't think about it anymore or the lump in her stomach would move up to her throat.

A tap on her shoulder brought her back to the

immediate reality of algebra. "Hey, Susan," Benny Morris whispered from the desk behind her. "How'd you do?"

Susan turned around slightly in her seat and wrinkled her nose. "Bad news."

"A C?"

"Worse."

"Let's see!" Benny bent forward to reach for Susan's paper but she slapped her hand down on top of it to cover the grade.

"Never mind," she said, feeling ashamed. Benny's grades were always better than hers.

"I got an A-minus," he gloated.

"Lucky you," Susan said with a sigh.

She looked down at the runner's watch her father had given her for her fifteenth birthday last year. 2:28. Just two minutes until the school day ended.

Part of Susan could hardly wait for class to be over so she could get out of here and get home. But another part dreaded the bell. It meant a confrontation with Miss Taylor, something Susan would be glad to wait years for. It meant getting bawled out or at least being lectured to about the importance of good grades.

Susan knew that sort of speech by heart. Her father, a history professor, gave her the same talk every time she brought home a report card. He always intended to be inspiring but Susan usually just ended up depressed. It didn't help that her sister Amy had never gotten lower than a B in her whole life. Susan knew her own grades could only look all the worse in comparison.

When the bell rang, the rest of the class

whipped shut their notebooks, stuffed their books and papers into their backpacks, and raced for the door. It was the end of the day and no one could wait to get outside into the late April sunshine.

Susan looked at their happy faces with envy. She picked up her test and pencil at a snail's pace, dragging out the time until she had to talk to Miss Taylor. Finally, after opening and closing the rings of her notebook three times to put in one last sheet of paper, Susan had no choice but to admit she was packed up and ready to go.

The room seemed terribly empty and silent. Susan stood up, raised her chin high, and walked slowly toward Miss Taylor's desk.

"Well, Susan," her teacher said, scrutinizing her through round gold-rimmed glasses. "You certainly didn't do well on your test."

Susan cleared her throat to prepare to defend herself. "I should have studied harder," she admitted weakly.

"Did you study at all?"

"A couple of hours."

"That should have been enough to pass the test." Miss Taylor tapped her pen on the desk briskly. "Didn't you understand the problems, Susan?"

"Yes. . . . Well, no. I guess not. I mean I must not have or I would have gotten a better grade." Susan studied the stitching around the toes of her loafers, her cheeks pink with unhappiness and embarrassment.

"Why did you do so badly then?" Miss Taylor asked, her voice softening. "Is anything wrong?"

Susan had the feeling Miss Taylor was referring to her personal life, but she didn't know exactly what to say. She looked up at her teacher again and shrugged. "I guess I've been kind of distracted lately."

"By what?"

"We just moved. Lots of stuff is going on."

"A move is always hard," Miss Taylor said gently. "Do you think Amy could help you with your homework?"

"I guess so," said Susan without conviction. She was sure Amy had enough to do in her accelerated math and science classes without having to help her sister.

"No." Miss Taylor shook her head decisively, as if she'd read Susan's mind. "No, that's not such a good idea. Brothers and sisters don't usually make the best tutors for each other, but you do need someone who can spend a fair amount of time with you. Pulling up this grade is going to take some work. H-m-m-m." Miss Taylor pressed her lips together as she thought. "I've got it," she said, her face brightening. "Colin Edwards."

"Who?"

"Colin is a junior and one of my best students. He has a lot of tutoring experience — he does it after school for extra credit."

"I don't know him," Susan said doubtfully.

Miss Taylor smiled. "You will in a minute. He's supposed to be here now to talk about the next Computer Club meeting. He's president this semester. A very bright boy."

Susan imagined a boy with his pants pulled up too high and two-inch-thick glasses. His eyes would probably squint from looking at a computer screen for hours at a time. A guy who'd make Benny Morris look like a prince.

"Would you be interested in working with him?" Miss Taylor asked, businesslike once more.

"Well. . . ." Susan stalled for an answer. She wasn't exactly thrilled at the prospect of spending afternoons going over algebra equations with a nerd. But when she looked down at her notebook and thought about her test with its red-penciled F practically burning through the paper, she knew she didn't have a choice. "I guess that would be okay," she said, resigned.

"Good!" Miss Taylor said. "We'll ask Colin and see if he agrees."

Just then the door swung open and Susan turned her head, her silky ponytail swinging. She stopped herself just in time from gasping out loud. This guy couldn't possibly be her tutor. He was by far the cutest boy she'd ever seen.

She took everything in in one quick, wide-eyed glance. He was tall, maybe six feet, with sandy blond hair and broad shoulders. His eyes were such a light, bright blue she could tell the color even from a distance — even through his gold-rimmed glasses.

Susan decided she actually liked his glasses, and she liked the way he dressed, too — definitely preppy in khaki slacks and a blue, button-down oxford cloth shirt. She liked his whole manner — he looked confident enough to do anything he set his mind to. Self-assurance showed as much in his walk as in the way his eyes twinkled when he smiled, and he was smiling as he approached

6

Miss Taylor's desk. As Susan watched him, she forgot to breathe a few times. Her heart was beating as if she'd just run five miles, at a dead sprint.

"Colin," Miss Taylor greeted him. "I want you to meet someone."

Susan couldn't help smiling. "Hi, Colin," she said brightly.

"This is Susan Atkinson," Miss Taylor said.

"You're Amy's sister, aren't you?" he asked, sitting casually on top of one of the desks in the front row.

"Uh-huh."

"We've had lots of classes together."

If he's an example of the kind of guy in Amy's accelerated math and science classes, Susan thought, then studying hard enough to get into them would definitely be worth it!

"Susan's having problems with algebra, Colin," Miss Taylor explained. "Would you be willing to tutor her for a while, until she gets her grade back up?"

"Sure," Colin said and smiled at Susan. "I'd be glad to."

"Could you start Monday?" Miss Taylor asked.

"No reason why not," Colin responded with an easygoing shrug.

"Is that okay with you, Susan?"

"It's great!" Susan exclaimed, then wondered if she'd sounded too enthusiastic. People weren't exactly supposed to be thrilled about needing a tutor. She tried to put a serious expression back on her face.

"Susan needs help with word problems," Miss Taylor continued. "You could start by going over her homework and explaining how to set up the equations."

"Sounds fine to me." Colin nodded.

"Me, too," Susan agreed.

Colin's blue eyes met Susan's blue eyes, and Susan hoped hers made half the impression on him that his did on her. "Should we get together at school or at your house?" he asked.

Susan thought quickly. Where could they get to know each other better? "How about my house?" she suggested. He gave her a thumbs-up sign. "Your house it is."

Susan wrote her address on a piece of notebook paper and handed it to Colin, who glanced at it before putting it into his pocket. "Hey, that's just two blocks from me. I live on Maple Avenue," he said cheerfully.

For the first time since the family moved, Susan was glad they had. The new neighborhood had a lot more going for it than it did ten minutes ago! She pictured herself walking home after school with Colin, holding hands, and talking about what they'd done that day. . . . If only there were a chance that picture could come to life, Susan thought hopefully.

As she headed out the door, she waved goodbye to Colin and Miss Taylor, her eyes glowing, and her feet ready to dance. She'd never been so glad to get an F in all her life.

Chapter
2

Dee hurried down the hall to get to Fiona's locker before her friend left for home. She glanced longingly at the many open windows. It was a gorgeous, sunny day. The hallway was packed with kids rushing to get outside. Like everyone else at Kennedy High, Dee had a bad case of spring fever, but she was stuck inside for a while longer.

She still had a lot to do before leaving for the day, and the most important task was working out a few more details for Marc's birthday party. He'd be seventeen on Sunday, and Dee had arranged for all their friends to meet at her house Saturday night after Marc's soccer game.

For the past two weeks she'd been inviting people and making arrangements in secret so the party would be a surprise for Marc. Kim was going to handle the food, although Dee intended to bake a cake for Marc herself. It might not turn out as elegant as one from Earthly Delights, Kim's mom's catering company, but it would have a lot of love in it. Fiona and Pamela had promised to help her make the decorations, and Peter Lacey had said he'd be disc jockey for the night and bring so many records they could dance for a week without hearing the same song twice. All the sneaking around should pay off in a great party.

Dee was feeling pressured about getting everything done in time, but also very excited as she rushed along the hall, barely noticing people she passed. She still had to see Kim and Fiona to make a few arrangements and then she had to do some work for *The Red and the Gold*. Her homework — and her spring fever — would just have to wait.

Dee reached Fiona's locker just as her friend was slamming the metal door shut.

"What a beautiful day!" Fiona exclaimed. "I can hardly wait to ride home on my bike."

"I wish I could go with you," Dee said wistfully.

"Staying late today?"

"I have to take photos of two girls on the track team."

"Who?"

"Liz Arnold and Janice Baker. They both won first place in their event at the state prelims."

Fiona shook her blonde head. "I don't know them."

Dee shrugged. "They're nice. Both seniors."

Fiona tied her backpack closed and slung it over one shoulder. She and Dee started down the

10

hall toward the exit to the parking lot. After they'd gotten away from the crowd, Fiona looked around carefully to make sure Marc wasn't in sight and then leaned closer to Dee.

"Is everything ready for Saturday?" Her British accent came through even when she whispered.

Just thinking about how much she still had left to do made Dee's heart beat faster as if she was at one of her dancercise classes. "I have to talk to Kim about the food in a minute, and I still have a lot of shopping to do. I haven't even bought one of Marc's presents yet!" she groaned.

"What are you giving him?"

"A blown-up picture I took of him and his family at Christmas. I already have that, but then I want to get him a pocket calculator, too." She laughed. "He wants one that's solar-powered. What a nerd, huh? I'm not sure what kind to get, though."

"Maybe Dick Westergard would have some idea," Fiona suggested.

"I was thinking of asking him," Dee said.

"I'd do it. I bet he'd go with you to buy one."

"Good idea." Dee nodded. "I'll call him when I get home. Maybe we could get together tomorrow after school. That means just one more thing to do!"

Dee sighed and pushed her short, ash-blonde hair back from her face as she bent down for a quick drink at the water fountain. She was still breathless from her sprint after the final bell.

"We've got to get busy on the decorations," she said, straightening up again. "Any ideas?"

"Jeremy brought a huge piece of paper home

11

from the art department yesterday so we could make a giant 'Happy Birthday' sign."

"Great," said Dee enthusiastically. "If I got balloons and crepe paper, we could string them up around the living room Saturday afternoon."

"Want me to bring flowers for the table?"

"Could you?"

"Sure. There are already some blooming in our garden. I'll pick a big bouquet." Fiona shifted her heavy backpack to her other shoulder and smiled at her friend. "I can't wait to see Marc when he walks in."

Dee nodded in agreement. All week long she'd been imagining how surprised he'd be. She could just see his expression when he found the whole crowd hiding in the kitchen waiting for him. His perpetual smile would break into a grin, and his warm blue eyes would crinkle at the corners with laughter. Looking forward to that one moment had kept Dee going through all the endless details and planning.

But during the past few days she'd started to worry a little, and not just over what flavor frosting would be best on Marc's cake. Marc seemed kind of distant lately, and Dee had no idea what might be on his mind. For a while she'd thought he suspected something about the party, but that didn't really make sense. If that were the case, he'd probably bend over backward to act like there was nothing out of the ordinary on his mind.

Dee wrinkled her forehead. "You don't think Marc knows anything about the party, do you?" she asked.

"No way," Fiona said firmly. "After lunch I

asked him what you were doing Saturday night and he said he was going to your house to watch a movie. He sounded incredibly innocent and unsuspecting."

"I told him I wanted to rent *Raiders of the Lost Ark* again."

"Well, he's all ready for it."

The two girls giggled. "For just a few more days, we've got to make sure he doesn't find out," Dee concluded.

"Make sure who doesn't find out what?" a boy's voice asked behind them.

Dee froze in her steps. She didn't have to turn around to realize that Marc had walked up behind her and Fiona without their knowing it. Her mouth went dry and she wished she could take a giant step backward and swallow those last words. She threw Fiona a desperate glance as she turned to face Marc.

Trying to look calm, Dee reached up and kissed Marc lightly on the cheek just as she always did when they met.

"Hi, Marc," Fiona said, her eyes a little too wide and her voice a little too loud.

"What were you guys talking about?" Marc asked again as they continued down the hall together.

Dee searched her mind frantically for something to say. All she could think of was how hard it was to keep a secret from someone she loved. That thought wouldn't move over to make room for even the tiniest of white lies.

"We weren't talking about anything important." Fiona came quickly and coolly to the rescue. "Just that I hope Mr. Henderson doesn't find out I had biology in England. He'd expect me to get A-pluses on all his tests."

Dee gave her friend a grateful smile. "Mr. Henderson would ask a lot more of her if he knew." She put in her two cents hoping to make their story more believable.

She watched his face carefully for a reaction. Marc looked at Fiona a bit oddly and then his blue eyes went straight to Dee's. She squirmed inside as she returned his gaze, trying to look completely truthful.

"I've been looking all over for you, Dee," Marc said simply after an awkward pause.

So he was going to let the subject drop. "How come?" Dee asked, letting her breath out in relief.

"I just went to the gym and found out Coach Howard had to go out of town. There's no game today. Probably not one tomorrow, either."

"No game?" She pretended to be thrilled. Marc would expect her to spend the afternoon with him. How was she going to meet Kim?

Fiona realized Dee's predicament. "Shouldn't you be out running around the track to stay in shape?" she asked casually.

"Naw, I played tennis with my brother yesterday." Marc put an arm firmly around Dee's shoulders and gave her a squeeze. "I mean it's not our real season, or anything, so it doesn't matter if we miss a game or practice. These pick-up games are just to keep in shape for fall — and for fun."

"Great," Fiona said, her voice as flat as day-old ginger ale.

As they approached the exit to the parking lot, Fiona turned away.

"I've got to get going," she said, throwing Dee a sympathetic look. "Talk to you later, Dee. See ya, Marc."

"Sure," Dee said, wishing with all her might that Marc would leave for home now, too.

No such luck. He held her even closer to his side as they continued down the hall. Normally Dee loved walking like this with Marc. She loved his touch, and the time they spent together was the happiest time she knew. But today all she could think about was Kim waiting for her outside the newspaper office. Kim's mother was going to shop that afternoon, so they had to make final decisions now about refreshments for the party. With Marc hanging around, it was definitely going to be difficult.

"Is Fiona failing biology?" Marc asked.

"Fiona?" said Dee without thinking. "No, she does well in everything." Then she remembered the story they made up about Mr. Henderson. "I mean. . . . Well, she's worrying a little about her grade, that's all."

"Wouldn't her transcript say she'd had biology? Why would they make her take it again?"

"Well . . ." Dee stalled, and then continued feebly. "That's a good point. Maybe there's been a mistake."

To her own ears this conversation sounded ridiculous, and it must have to Marc, too. Dee felt him looking down at her, but she didn't have the nerve to meet his eyes.

"Dee, is anything wrong?" Marc asked, his voice concerned.

"Wrong?" she echoed vaguely.

"You seem really uptight."

"I'm okay." Dee shrugged. "I guess I've just got lots on my mind."

"Like what?" He stopped walking and she was forced to stop, too. He turned her toward him, keeping his arms affectionately around her.

"Oh, nothing really." Dee avoided his gaze by focusing on the collar of his letter jacket.

Marc's forehead wrinkled up into a frown. "I can tell something's going on in that head of yours! What's bothering you? You know you can tell me."

"Nothing," Dee insisted, too emphatically. "I've just got things to do today. You know, pictures, homework."

Marc sounded disappointed and a little irritated. "I thought we could get a Coke at the sub shop."

"I wish I could," Dee said honestly. "But I'm supposed to take some photos this afternoon."

Dee felt Marc's arms tense around her. She gulped and finally looked up at him. He was scowling.

"Fine," he said crisply. His eyes were narrowed and cool. "That's just fine."

"What do you mean?" Dee asked, surprised by his anger.

"Nothing," he said sarcastically. Dee recognized an imitation of her own evasiveness.

When he dropped his arms from her shoulders, she felt suddenly exposed and lonely.

"I'm really sorry, Marc," she said. And she was sorry. The look on his face went right to her heart and made it ache. But she didn't have time to soothe him right now. Half her thoughts were still on Kim, and after all, Marc's party was the whole reason she was acting strangely. He just didn't know it. "I've just got a lot of things to do today," she repeated.

"Sure," Marc said. "Well, it was great spending the afternoon with you." Without another word, he turned on his heel and started back toward the door where they'd just left Fiona.

"Marc?" Dee called after him. He must be more upset than she'd thought. She couldn't leave like this, even if it meant making something up.

"Forget it, Dee," Marc waved a hand dismissively. "See you tomorrow."

Dee stood frozen in place and watched his broad, muscular back move down the hall away from her. What's going on? she wondered, confused. Marc had never acted like this toward her before. His tone had been like a slap in the face.

Sure, she'd been a little distracted and out of it, but ordinarily Marc would just shrug and laugh. But instead he'd said "See you tomorrow." Did that mean he wasn't going to call her tonight? They'd talked on the phone every single night since they'd started going together last November. Something must be on his mind, Dee decided. I'm not the only one who's keeping a secret. And whatever it is, it can't be good.

Dee didn't have time just then to think about

the scene that had just taken place with Marc. She was confused and hurt but she pushed those feelings out of her mind. She shook herself, both mentally and physically, and headed for *The Red and the Gold* office, already late to meet Kim.

She found Kim standing patiently outside the office door.

"I thought you'd forgotten me!" Kim said with a friendly smile as Dee hurried toward her.

"Marc's soccer game was canceled today," Dee explained. "He wanted to do something together."

"What'd you tell him?"

"That I had to take photos, which is half true."

"Poor Dee," Kim said sympathetically. "It's hard to plan a whole party in secret."

"No kidding." Dee sighed. "I was just thinking that. Leading a double life is starting to wear on my nerves."

She and Kim found the office empty. They sat down at one end of the long conference table at the back of the room. A bulletin board haphazardly covered with yellow slips of paper detailing Sasha's editorial assignments filled the wall behind them.

"Have you decided what kind of cake you're going to bake yet?" Kim took a scribbled shopping list out of her backpack.

Dee tipped her chair back and rested her head against the bulletin board. "I was thinking chocolate. Marc loves it." She giggled. "And so do I! Although I don't get to eat it much these days since my diet."

"I know, I should stay away from it myself. How about making two layers and putting some cherry filling between them?" Kim suggested.

"Good idea! And I thought I'd write something original like 'Happy Birthday, Marc' in icing on top."

"You could put a soccer goal on each end."

"Perfect!" Dee laughed.

Kim tapped her pencil eraser against the table as she thought. "I've got a great recipe for miniature pizzas I'm thinking of making. And maybe some popcorn with parmesan cheese."

Dee nodded. "We could have the chips and salty stuff first and save the cake till later, maybe around ten o'clock." She pictured Marc's face as she walked toward him with a big cake sparkling with birthday candles. "Marc'll love it!" She clapped her hands together happily.

She and Kim went over the rest of the list — chips, raw vegetables, and two special Earthly Delights dips Kim claimed Woody would die for. For beverages, they'd stock a couple of cases of soda, "And a few cartons of milk," Kim added. "You've got to have it with birthday cake!"

"I've got the money here to pay the deposit." Dee pulled her wallet from the pocket of her oversized cardigan sweater jacket. "My mom'll give you the rest Friday night if that's okay?"

"Sure," Kim said. She put away the bills Dee gave her. "Marc hasn't found out anything about all this, has he?"

"No, but Fiona and I just had a close call." Dee described her recent encounter with Marc in the hall.

"He probably fell for your story," Kim said reassuringly. "Even if he didn't, he wouldn't necessarily think anything about a party. Woody talked to him at lunch and asked him what he was doing Saturday night and — "

Dee interrupted her with a groan. "Oh, no."

Kim raised her eyebrows. "What's wrong?"

"Fiona asked him the same thing. He'll start to suspect something if everybody starts bugging him about Saturday!"

"Don't worry, Dee." Kim laughed and patted her arm. "I'll tell Woody to spread the word so nobody else mentions Saturday, okay?"

"Okay," Dee said. Keeping this party a surprise was turning out to be more complicated than she'd ever imagined.

Kim looked at her watch and gathered up her things. "I've got to find Mom," she said.

"Thanks for all your help with this, Kim."

"Hey, no problem!"

After Kim left, Dee waited alone for a few minutes for the two girls on the track team to show up. She paced nervously around the office and wished Sasha were there. She needed someone to talk to.

If Marc suspected anything about the party, Dee would be really disappointed, but she could deal with it. His behavior that afternoon just didn't make sense, though. He hadn't been teasing, he'd been mad.

Dee hitched one slim hip up on the edge of the conference table, her face thoughtful — and confused. It just wasn't like him to react so

20

strongly to her not being able to go somewhere with him. He was usually more easygoing — their whole relationship had always been lighthearted. Dee folded her arms tightly, suddenly chilled despite the warm sun beaming in the window.

Chapter
3

"Amy! Amy! Guess what!"

Susan tore up the stairs to her sister's bedroom with their dachshund Sam chasing her on his short, bowed legs. When she got to the landing, she skidded on her mother's favorite Oriental rug.

Flinging open the bedroom door, Susan found Amy sitting at her desk, surrounded by cardboard boxes. Her bed was covered with a white counterpane spread, and white lace curtains hung at the windows. There weren't any pictures on the walls yet, or books in the cases near her closet. Amy's cherished stereo wasn't even hooked up yet.

"Amy!" Susan shouted again at her sister, a big grin on her face. "I just got an F on my algebra test and — "

"An F?" Amy interrupted, horrified.

"It's really not as bad as it sounds," Susan assured her. "Besides, something wonderful has happened because of it."

Susan whirled around and landed on Amy's bed. Panting, Sam tried a few leaps to jump up beside her. When he couldn't make the distance on his own, she reached down and hauled him up.

"*What* are you talking about?" Amy asked, completely baffled.

"I got an F," Susan repeated. "And so Miss Taylor asked me to see her after class." Susan described in minute detail each step that led to her meeting Colin. "I can't believe he's going to be my tutor," she said finally, her blue eyes dreamy. "He's the most gorgeous guy I ever saw. I had a crush on him instantly. I just have to get him to ask me out!"

"Wait a minute." Amy assumed the slightly stern, older-sister manner she often used with Susan, and Susan's face took on the slightly resentful, younger-sister pout with which she often responded. The sisters had had this kind of conversation before.

Susan, the younger sister, was bubbly and cute — exactly what Amy wasn't, although they did look a lot alike, with the same silky blonde hair and deep blue eyes. But Amy had a special quality about her, a gentle seriousness that drew people to her. She was pretty rather than cute, and on the quiet side, in complete contrast to her carefree, energetic sister.

"You just met Colin," Amy pointed out, her voice mild. "You can't already be talking about *dating* him."

23

"Yes, I can," Susan insisted stubbornly. "I've never wanted to go out with anyone so much in my life!" She flipped off her shoes and pulled her long, slim legs up onto Amy's bed. "Do you know Colin at all?"

"Just a little," Amy said. "He's been in all my math and science classes. I think he's pretty good friends with Marc Harrison, and he hangs out a lot with people in the Computer Club."

"He's president of the Computer Club," Susan informed her. "Why didn't you ever tell me about him?"

Amy smiled at her sister's enthusiasm. "I didn't know you'd be so interested!" she said. "I really don't know him that well, anyway. Our classes are pretty intense — we don't exactly sit around passing notes."

Susan leaned back against her sister's pillow, half closing her long-lashed eyes. "I'd find a way to get to know him even if we were taking the most advanced physics class in the universe!"

Amy shook her head and laughed. Susan had always been a boy-crazy flirt. She really couldn't say she was surprised she'd fallen for her algebra tutor, of all people. "You'd better get serious about your grade," she warned good-naturedly. "That's more important than having a date with Colin."

"Yeah, yeah," Susan agreed. "But don't you think it's great to have him for a tutor?" She grinned, "I think I'll like algebra more if it's a little romantic."

"For sure. I really hope things work out for you, Suze."

Susan gave Sam a pat on his nose, then reached over and grabbed the pink stuffed rabbit lying on Amy's bed. She put it in her lap and rested her chin on its head. The rabbit's ears flopped to each side of Susan's flushed cheeks.

Her face gradually became more serious. "When I first saw that F, I thought about what would happen if Mom found out."

"Or Dad." Amy rolled her eyes. "He'd hit the ceiling."

"I know. But I'll get the grade back up. Don't worry."

"I know you will." Amy reached over and squeezed Susan's foot affectionately. "It's been hard on you with all the changes."

"You, too," Susan said. She rubbed her chin against the furry pink fabric of the rabbit's head and looked at the jungle of unpacked cartons in the center of Amy's room. "It'll be good to get settled," she added with a sigh. Looking at all those boxes made her feel displaced and uprooted.

Amy followed her gaze. "I'm sure tired of this chaos, that's for sure."

"Mom said she'd help me unpack my room this weekend," Susan said.

"Want me to help you now?" Amy offered.

"No, thanks. I could put it off for a hundred years."

"Not me. I can't stand bumping into boxes!"

Amy grabbed one of the cartons and tugged off the tape across its top. She reached inside, pulled out a small stack of books, and set them neatly on her book shelf.

Susan watched her sister put her photo album

on the shelf. "Let's see that," she said, holding out her hand.

After Amy gave it to her, Susan started flipping slowly through the pages. "This one of Mom and Dad with Sam last summer is really good," she said, her head bent so close over the photograph that her ponytail fell over the page.

Amy stepped over a few boxes so she could look down at the picture over her sister's shoulder. "Remember how Sam made friends with that dog on the beach that was ten times his size? That day was so much fun."

"Yeah." Susan nodded, still staring at the photograph. She studied it a few moments longer, then looked up at Amy, her blue eyes brimming with tears. "Do you think Mom and Dad will ever get back together?"

"I wish they would. But I don't think so," Amy said softly. "Mom says they'll always be good friends, though."

"She just says that so we won't worry." Susan shook her head, disbelieving.

"They'll keep in touch. We don't have to worry that Dad'll disappear. I really believe that."

Amy's calm and soothing voice made her sister feel just a little better. "I sure miss him," Susan said, turning to another page in the album. Every time she thought about how her father wasn't living with them anymore, her stomach tied itself into a knot.

"Me, too," Amy agreed.

"I wish he'd move back."

"I guess he won't since we're in this little house. He wouldn't have his study anymore."

26

"He could grade his papers at the university," Susan said hopefully.

"He wouldn't, though." Amy reached into the box for another handful of books. "I guess there's no point wishing things were different."

Susan didn't say anything, but she sniffled. Amy glanced at the books in her hands, then over toward her sister. "Don't worry, Suze. We'll get used to it. We can always go stay with Dad in D.C. whenever we want. We haven't lost him."

"I know," Susan said, without much conviction.

"I wish I could make everything better for you." Amy sighed.

Susan jumped up and impulsively hugged her sister. "You do. You've helped me so much."

Amy smiled at Susan gratefully. She pulled a poster out of one of the boxes. The paper was rolled up tightly with a rubber band. "Help me a minute, would you?" she asked.

Susan spread the poster out against the wall while Amy stepped back to view it critically. The poster, a field of poppies in the sunshine, brightened the room immediately, making a sharp contrast to the seriousness of their conversation.

"Move it to the left," Amy said.

"How's this?"

"Perfect!" Amy opened her desk drawer and started shuffling through it for thumb tacks.

"My arms are getting tired," Susan moaned.

"Here." Amy stuck a tack at each corner of the poster. "Looks great, huh?"

"Even Mom would approve," Susan agreed. Their mother was an interior decorator, and she never hesitated to suggest changes for their rooms if something didn't quite please her fastidious eye.

Susan flopped back down on the bed and started looking through the album again. As she turned the pages, she started to fidget. Some of the pictures bothered her. They brought back memories of so many happy times that would never happen again.

"Do you get sad?" she asked suddenly, looking up at her sister.

"You mean about Mom and Dad?"

"Uh-huh."

"Sure," Amy said.

"It's even worse right now, since we moved," Susan observed.

"I know." Amy nodded agreement. "But I guess we'll get used to it," she said practically.

Susan looked back at the album for a moment, then closed it abruptly and swung her legs over the side of the bed to stand up. "There's *some* good in what's happened," she said, her face brightening into an impish grin.

"What's that?" Amy looked puzzled.

"We moved, and Colin lives just two blocks away on Maple Avenue. He told me so today!"

"And now you'll run into him everywhere you go!"

"You bet."

Amy laughed. "You'll probably go nuts from anticipation before your first tutoring session even rolls around."

"I know." Susan smiled ruefully.

"When is it, anyway?"

"Monday after school."

28

Just as Amy leaned down to rip open the box that held her microscope, the phone rang in the hall outside her bedroom.

"Maybe it's Colin," Amy teased.

"I wish!"

When she returned a few seconds later Susan put on a sorrowful face which was hard to do since she was giggling. "No, it wasn't Colin." She sighed dramatically and fell back on the bed next to Sam like a wounded opera star. "It's Dee."

Amy went to answer the phone, laughing. She and Dee had been friends since last fall when they worked together on a science project, and they talked on the phone regularly. Dee was one of the few people Amy had confided in when she'd first heard about her parents' plan to divorce, and Dee had been very supportive.

"What's up?" Dee asked in greeting.

"Oh, I'm unpacking books and talking to Susan. She's gone temporarily berserk." Amy wound the telephone cord around her finger and winked at Susan, who'd poked her head around the corner and now stuck out her tongue.

"Want to go for a bike ride?" Dee was saying.

"It's kind of late. My mom'll be home in a few minutes."

"There's still half an hour till dinner," Dee urged.

It sounded to Amy as if Dee had something on her mind. "Is anything wrong?" she asked, concerned.

Dee hesitated. "I'm not sure. I want to see what you think."

29

It wasn't like Dee to sound so worried. Amy made up her mind quickly.

"Okay, I'll be there in about five minutes," she said and hung up the receiver.

She went to her bedroom door and found Susan pouring over the photo album again. "Tell Mom I'll be back by six-thirty, okay?"

She hurried downstairs, got her bicycle out of the garage, and started off along the street.

Chapter
4

The afternoon sun was getting low in the sky as Amy pedaled toward Dee's house. It sent warm golden shafts through the leaves of the trees that lined the neighborhood streets.

Amy glanced a little regretfully at the large, stately houses she was passing. Just a little over a week ago, she'd lived in one only a few blocks from Dee. She'd loved the huge screened-in porch, the broad green lawn, the extra bedrooms where guests could sleep on weekends.

But then her mother had announced they'd have to move. "We don't need so much room with your father gone," she'd said. "And there's no point making payments on such a big place."

Amy knew she'd always miss that house. She'd lived there since she was a very little girl, as long as she could remember. The past week had been so strange, waking up in a new bedroom and looking out the window at an unfamiliar view.

It would probably take months until she could find her way to the bathroom at night in the dark without running into walls, and years until she felt she really belonged in the new place.

As she shifted her bicycle gear and turned the corner onto a quiet side street, she wondered if Susan would always miss their old house, too. In some ways Susan had taken their parents' divorce even harder than Amy had. Susan usually covered up her feelings with a carefree approach to life, but deep down she was as sensitive as Amy, and maybe even more vulnerable.

Thinking about her sister brought Colin Edwards to mind. Even though Amy didn't know Colin very well, just from seeing him in classes she suspected he might be good for Susan. Almost any boyfriend could distract her from her sadness and be there while she got over their family's problems, but Colin seemed really responsible. And everyone knew how smart he was — he might even be able to get Susan to study harder and get her grades back up. Colin was certainly more serious than most of the guys Susan had crushes on. Amy did hope something would happen between him and Susan.

She turned onto Dee's street and saw her friend waiting in front of her house. Dee was leaning against her bicycle, ready to take off the minute Amy arrived.

"That was fast," Dee said with a smile. "It seems like I just hung up the phone!"

Dee hopped on her bike and the two pedaled slowly down the street. A cool breeze blew in their faces. The street was quiet except for an occasional car — someone on their way home from work.

"So what's going on?" Amy glanced at Dee through wind-swept blonde wisps.

Dee frowned, trying to decide where to begin. "It's Marc," she said finally.

"There's nothing wrong, is there?" Amy asked.

"I can't tell," Dee admitted. "He was so weird this afternoon. I've never seen him act this way."

"Maybe he thinks something's going on. You're so involved with his party."

"He doesn't suspect a thing about the party as far as I can tell. Or at least I hope he doesn't." Dee explained how Marc had come up behind her and Fiona and overheard what they'd said.

"Whew!" Amy exhaled. "That was close."

Dee shifted her gears with a metallic click. "Let's go to Rose Hill Park," she suggested.

Dee was in the lead as the girls headed north along the winding road. Amy rode as close to Dee's back wheel as she could so that they could talk.

"In what way's Marc being weird?" she shouted up to her.

"Now that I think about it, something's been wrong for at least a week. He's been kind of distant. And today he got mad without that much of a reason," Dee shouted back.

She explained how Marc had acted when she couldn't go to the sub shop. As she talked, she started feeling a bit annoyed herself. She was trying so hard to get ready for Marc's birthday, and he didn't even appreciate her efforts. Of course, she knew rationally that he couldn't appreciate what she was doing because he didn't know about the party. But couldn't he at least realize how much she cared for him and how hard she was trying to make him happy?

"Did Marc really seem angry?" Amy asked. "Or was he just hurt that you wouldn't take a few minutes out to get a Coke with him?"

"More mad, I think." Dee clenched her fists around her handlebars as she started pedaling up the hill. "I just don't understand, Amy."

"It probably doesn't matter, Dee," Amy said. "There must be some misunderstanding."

"Then why would he get mad all of a sudden?" Dee insisted.

"Maybe he's frustrated because soccer's over," Amy suggested. "Maybe the off-season practicing and pick-up games aren't enough. Marc is too competitive for this casual, laid-back playing."

"But he says he's excited about summer coming. He just got a job at the Rose Hill Computer Store and he and Ted and some of the other guys are going to play baseball again. They'll practice nearly every night. I'll probably see even less of him than I do now."

"Then he can't be upset about soccer," Amy agreed. "Frankly, I don't have any other ideas. You know Marc better than I do!"

Dee laughed. "I thought so; But now I'm wondering if something's bothering him and I don't even know it," she said.

"You mean something having nothing to do with your keeping secrets about the party?"

Dee turned her head and nodded back at Amy.

"Yeah. I wonder if it's just plain something to do with *me*."

"All you've been thinking about is his birthday. Once he walks in on Saturday and sees all the work you've done, it'll blow his mind. You'll see," Amy said comfortingly. "He'll be crazier about you than ever. You don't have anything to worry about."

The two girls rode through the iron gate that led to Rose Hill Park. The trees and bushes had turned a darker green in the twilight. Long shadows made graceful, curving patterns on the street. Amy and Dee turned cautiously onto a gravel road and pedaled side by side in silence.

"What do you think I should do, Amy?" Dee asked finally.

"Talk to him. That's all you can do. You'll feel better right away."

"Maybe he'll act like nothing's wrong."

"Even if he does, you have to try. Everything should be out in the open in a good relationship."

What Amy said made sense. Dee started to think she must be overreacting. After the party, everything would be fine. But in the meantime, she wouldn't be able to get Marc off her mind.

"Do you think I should wait for *him* to bring up what's bugging him?" she asked Amy.

Amy shook her head. "You should try and work things out when they're happening," she said firmly. "If you wait, things just build up."

"I guess I'm not exactly sure how to handle it," Dee admitted. "You probably think I'm acting silly, but to tell you the truth, this is the first time

35

we've ever even come close to an argument. It's just thrown me for a loop."

"I don't think you're silly at all," Amy said kindly. "And it should be easy to get this weight off your mind. Next time you talk to him, tell him you have something to say, and just say what you've said to me!"

It did sound so easy. "You're right," Dee said, sitting up straighter and tossing her head back with determination. "Okay, I'll do it!"

"Good." Amy smiled at her friend, and then laughed. "If we've got that settled, we can head home. I don't want to be late for dinner and get Mom upset!"

The two girls turned a corner to go back. Amy squeezed her hand brakes too early, and before she realized what was happening, the bike started to skid on the gravel.

"Watch out" Dee cried, too late. The back wheel of Amy's bicycle spun out quickly at an angle. With a crash, she and her bike landed in the road.

The pain that shot up Amy's leg was prickly for just a second, then changed to a horrible, hot ache.

"Are you all right?!" Dee shouted. She threw her own bike down and rushed toward her friend.

"I guess so," Amy said, her voice shaky.

Dee put a hand on Amy's shoulder. "Can you move?" she asked.

Amy shifted her left leg. It was stiff and it hurt like crazy. "Yeah, I think so," she said.

"Here, let's see." Dee carefully lifted up Amy's

bike and bent down to examine her friend's leg. Amy's cotton pants had a big rip in the knee and both her elbows were badly scraped.

"You've got some nasty cuts," Dee said. "But they don't look too bad."

"Maybe it'll just hurt for a little while," Amy moaned. "I *hope*."

"Can you stand up?"

"I think so."

Dee helped Amy slowly to her feet. Grimacing with pain, Amy hobbled toward her bike.

"I can go call one of my parents to come get us," Dee offered.

"That's too much trouble. If we go slowly, I can make it home. I think."

Dee touched her friend's shoulder gingerly, wishing she could help Amy feel better. "Can I do anything?" she asked. "Can you walk if you lean on me?"

Amy managed a wan smile. "Just don't tell anybody what a klutz I am!"

Amy leaned against her bike for a few minutes to catch her breath. She climbed on with the energy of an exhausted grandmother. She started off, wobbly at first, then a bit more steadily. Dee stuck close beside her.

"I can't believe I just did this," Amy said, shaking her head. "I feel like I got hit by a truck."

"We can stop at my house and fix you up before you go the rest of the way," Dee said. "I insist."

As they rode back to Dee's, Amy chattered to

distract herself from her stinging cuts and the way her left knee burned every time she pedaled it up toward her handlebars.

"Susan met Colin Edwards today. He's going to tutor her in math," she said between clenched teeth. "She's in love with him and it only took five minutes."

"Colin's really cute," Dee said. "But do you think he's Susan's type?"

"He is kind of studious," Amy agreed, "but you know what they say: Opposites attract."

"He and Marc are pretty good friends from the Computer Club," Dee said, keeping a concerned eye on her wounded friend.

"Is he going out with anybody?"

"Not that I know of."

"Well, maybe he'll fall for Susan the way she has for him. She needs somebody right now."

By the time they got to Dee's house, Amy's leg felt both stiffer and sturdier. Mrs. Patterson bandaged her cuts and offered to drive her home, but Amy assured her she could get back on her own.

It was dark when Amy cautiously started out again from Dee's driveway.

"I'll talk to Marc about everything tonight," Dee promised her friend as she waved good-bye from the front door.

Amy was late for dinner after all.

Chapter
5

"That must be Colin," Amy called to Susan as the doorbell rang.

"Can you answer it?" Susan shouted from her bedroom. "I'm not ready yet!"

Amy grimaced as she got up from her desk. Every time she'd moved her left leg that day she'd wished she'd never heard of such a thing as a bicycle, much less ridden one. The really bad pain had stopped by the time she woke up that morning, but her leg was still stiff and walking wasn't much fun. She'd had to hobble from class to class at Kennedy and by the time she'd gotten home she was exhausted.

Holding onto the banister to keep the weight off her leg, she hopped with a thump down one stair at a time. Sam's sniffing right at her heels didn't help much.

When he barked fiercely at the front door, Amy laughed. She was always amused by how such a small dog could consider himself such a tough protector.

Amy opened the door and found Colin grinning at her. "Hi! Is Susan here?" he asked between Sam's yaps.

Amy smiled a warm welcome back at him. "She'll be down in a second."

Amy, trying not to limp, led Colin slowly into the living room. Sam ran beside them sniffing at the cuffs of Colin's slacks.

"I saw your leg was hurt in class today," Colin said conversationally.

"Was it that obvious?" Amy asked, a little embarrassed.

"Only when you moved," Colin teased. "What happened?"

"I was bike riding with Dee Patterson and got into a wrestling match with a gravel road," Amy said sheepishly.

Colin wrinkled his nose in an expression of sympathy. "It hurts just hearing about it."

Amy nodded. "Not as bad as it hurt doing it."

Holding onto the upholstered arm for support, Amy began lowering herself slowly into the living room chair.

"Here, let me help you," Colin said quickly. He strode over to her and held her arm firmly while she eased herself down onto the soft, overstuffed pillows.

"Thanks." Amy gave him an appreciative smile. Colin's consideration made the stiffness in her leg seem not so bad somehow.

"Any time." Colin put his backpack on the

coffee table and sat down on the sofa across from her.

"Have you studied for our chemistry test tomorrow?" he asked.

"I just started an hour ago," Amy admitted.

"It shouldn't be too hard."

"I sure hope not," she said.

"Mr. Jessup's a pretty good guy."

"Did you see him yank the molecule chart off the wall by mistake yesterday?"

"Yeah. It almost bopped him on the head!" Colin leaned back against the sofa and laughed heartily with Amy. "Remember that day when he connected the gas hose to the water?"

"It was like a sprinkler on his desk," Amy laughed.

"He's definitely out-to-lunch sometimes."

"All the time!" Amy said, reaching down to pull Sam up beside her in the chair. "I guess I shouldn't laugh at him, though. My dad's a teacher and he says he has nightmares about doing stuff like that."

Colin leaned forward and rested his elbows on his knees. "What does your dad teach?" he asked, really looking interested.

"History."

"My dad's a physics professor."

"He can help you when we take that next year, then," Amy said.

"Let's hope I won't need any help," Colin said, his blue eyes twinkling.

Sam suddenly jumped down from Amy's lap and dashed for the door with more ferocious yaps.

"What's with him?" asked Colin.

Amy shrugged. "Probably just someone on the sidewalk. He's not used to living here yet."

"You just moved?"

"Last week."

"You'll like the neighborhood," Colin assured her enthusiastically. "I've been here since third grade."

Amy almost said she already knew he lived nearby, but she stopped herself. She didn't want Colin to find out Susan had told her everything he'd said.

"The park's great," Colin continued. "You can swim all summer if you don't mind mob scenes."

"Susan said there were tennis courts, too."

"Yeah." Colin glanced at his watch. "Is she out playing now?" His mischievous smile told Amy he was joking.

"I don't know what's keeping her," Amy said. "I sure hope you can help her. She's never been too thrilled about math."

"Why don't you tutor her?" Colin asked.

"Susan said Miss Taylor doesn't think family works too well together that way. You can probably be more objective with her than I could." Amy didn't add that once Susan set eyes on Colin she wouldn't have settled for anyone else, even if Albert Einstein had volunteered to tutor her.

"I hope so," Colin said, pushing his glasses up against the bridge of his nose. "I've been tutoring off and on for the last three years." He winked. "Only a few of my victims have flunked."

His grin was warm and friendly. Without even

thinking about it, Amy found herself smiling back with the same sunny intensity. It was hard not to respond to Colin's open, comfortable manner. It suddenly occurred to Amy that Susan would be lucky to have him for a boyfriend.

Just then Susan appeared at the foot of the stairs. Seeing her snapped Amy out of her brief reverie. Colin turned away from Amy to look at her sister. "Hi, Susan," he said.

Amy's eyes widened as her sister walked into the living room. She'd obviously just curled her hair — her ponytail bounced with a life of its own with her every step. Susan's lip gloss and blue eye shadow had been put on with such care, Amy suspected she'd been working on her makeup since she got home from school. Amy was most surprised, though, by Susan's outfit. Or rather, Amy's *newest* outfit — on Susan's body. Susan hadn't exactly asked permission before sneaking her sister's yellow miniskirt and sweater vest out of her closet. Amy was usually happy to trade clothes with Susan, but she couldn't keep from bristling with annoyance now.

"Great outfit, Susan," she said pointedly as Susan flashed Colin her most dazzling smile.

"Thanks," Susan said in all innocence.

Amy swallowed her irritation as best as she could. She tried to be more understanding of her sister. Susan probably needed the new clothes just to boost her morale. This was her first big chance to get to know Colin, and Amy shouldn't be selfish. Besides, after talking with Colin just now, Amy hoped more than ever that he'd fall for her sister. He was as wonderful as Susan had said.

Colin had gotten to his feet and now he smiled down at Susan. "We've got two hours to turn you into a math whiz," he said.

"Good luck," Amy said teasingly.

"Where'd you like to work, Colin?" Susan asked, ignoring her sister and blinking at Colin with incredibly long, thick lashes. "In here or the kitchen?"

Amy could tell it was time for her to make an exit.

"See you later," she said as she pulled herself up slowly from the chair. "I've got to study for our chem test."

"See ya," said Colin.

Amy sighed to herself as she made her way up the stairs slowly and painfully, in contrast to Susan's bouncy descent a few minutes ago. She told herself there was no reason to mind because Colin had transferred his attention so quickly and completely from her to Susan. He was Susan's tutor, after all.

But Amy couldn't help wishing, just for a moment, that she wasn't such a good student. It could be fun to get extra help from somebody like Colin Edwards.

"Come on into the kitchen," Susan said to Colin. "We can sit at the table and watch the birds at the feeder outside the window."

"Better to look at the algebra problems," Colin said with a crooked grin.

They got settled at the round oak table and Susan pulled her last algebra test tentatively from her notebook. Colin got out a piece of paper and a pencil.

"We'd better take a look at your test first to see where you need help," he said in a business-like voice.

Susan flinched. This was the moment she'd been dreading but she had to get it over with. Colin's going to think I'm the biggest dummy, she thought as she handed him the test.

"I know I didn't work hard enough," she said apologetically. She studied his handsome face for signs of disapproval and was relieved when she didn't see any.

"That's okay. What's important is that you start studying now," he said matter-of-factly, glancing over the test. "You've got to promise you'll take advantage of our time together. And you have to try to remember what I tell you when you're studying by yourself during the week."

"I promise," Susan said with a brilliant smile. Colin was sitting so close, she could almost feel the warmth coming from his body. She glanced at his arm, which looked strong underneath the pinstriped oxford shirt. She leaned in a little closer so their arms were nearly touching.

"Do you understand the mistakes you made on the test?" Colin asked her. Susan dragged her eyes back to the dull piece of paper on the table in front of her.

"Miss Taylor went over it in class this afternoon," she said.

"And you've got everything now?"

"I *think* so." Susan looked deep into his blue eyes.

"Then we can work on your homework for the week and get you studying for your test next Friday. Miss Taylor still has a test every week, doesn't she?"

"Uh-huh."

Colin opened Susan's algebra book and began explaining how to make equations from word problems. "You have to read them carefully first," he said. "And then you try and figure out an equation to stand for what the problem's asking. The trick is to choose a letter for the unknown and then fill out the equation with the numbers you do know."

Susan sighed. "Sure," she said, even though she hadn't understood a word he'd just said.

"Look at this one. If two trains are going down the track. . . ." Colin carefully read the first homework problem in Susan's book out loud. "Now what would x stand for?"

Susan blinked. As long as Colin was lecturing to her, everything was fine. He had no idea she wasn't following him. She wasn't prepared for him to ask her questions, however.

"Uh. . . ." She hesitated. "Well . . . x stands for the train track, right?"

"No. It's for the speed the second train is going." Colin looked at her to see if she understood. Susan tried to appear intelligent.

"This is what the equation would be," he said. When he reached for the pencil to write down the numbers, his hand brushed Susan's lightly. Her own hand tingled. All she could think of was the

46

wonderful sensation of his touch — the equation evaded her understanding completely.

But she was determined to make him think she was smart, so she forced herself to listen attentively to everything he said, nodding her head enthusiastically at regular intervals.

For a while he didn't ask her any more questions and Susan was safe in her state of mental fog. But the more Colin talked, the more she finally did start to understand, almost despite herself.

"I've got it!" she shouted spontaneously when he finished reading one of the last problems. "The x would be the length of the room!"

"Right!" Colin grinned at her. Like an affectionate older brother, he reached over and gave her ponytail a gentle yank. "You may be dense once in a while, but you do catch on eventually."

Susan beamed. She *was* glad to be getting the word problems finally. It was discouraging not to do well in school, and it gave her a good feeling when something clicked the way it just had with the algebra problem. But even better than that feeling was the way Colin had just touched her hair. She swished her ponytail across her shoulder, wishing her hair had nerves so she could feel where his hand had been.

"Now let's get you ready to study for the rest of the week," Colin said.

As he carefully wrote out exactly what she should read and what problems she should work out before Friday, Susan studied his hands. They looked strong, as if they should be dribbling a basketball down a court.

"I want you to go over these problems a hundred times if you have to before you take the test," Colin concluded. He put his notebook back into his knapsack. "And if there's anything you don't understand, call me." He wrote his phone number down on the back of Susan's test. "I can explain most things pretty well over the phone. Or you could always ask Amy for help."

"Okay," Susan said. She was already planning to fake not understanding something in a few days so she could call Colin and talk to him.

"You promise you'll study?" he asked.

"For sure," Susan said.

"I'll be disappointed if you don't." Colin gave her another one of his confident grins and got up from the table. Susan melted a little inside.

"Don't worry. I'll get an A-plus on the next test," she declared. She'd make an A at least — or die trying. If it were the last thing she ever did, she'd bring her grade back up. To impress Colin and to impress herself.

For a moment, Susan imagined telling him she'd gotten an A and watching a smile spread over his face. She wouldn't mind a congratulatory hug. But even better would be a hug and a kiss because he really cared about her. Maybe it would happen.

Her attention went back to Colin as he walked through the living room to the front door. They said good-bye and she watched him from the window as he disappeared down the street on his bicycle. Then she ran upstairs to Amy's bedroom.

"It's working!" Susan shouted as she pushed

open Amy's door with such force that the door knob slammed against the wall. "I think maybe he's starting to like me!"

"That's great, Suze," Amy said. "How about the algebra?"

"I got that today, too." Susan stood beside Amy's desk, excitedly raising herself up and down on her toes. "He's such a great tutor, Amy. I finally understood exactly how to work the problems."

"I'm glad," Amy said.

"I hope everything works out!"

"It'd be fantastic," she agreed. Holding her leg at an angle so it wouldn't hurt so much when she stood, Amy pulled herself up from the chair. "Let's go put the casserole in the oven before Mom gets home."

As Amy followed Susan and Sam downstairs to the kitchen, she decided she was very happy for her sister. She hoped Susan would get exactly what she wanted. Seeing her sister radiating excitement just now was sure better than all the days recently when she'd seemed so sad. And after talking to Colin this afternoon — it was hard to believe she'd had so many classes with him and they'd never really met — Amy had decided he was a pretty neat guy; Susan deserved someone like him.

Amy leaned on the banister and half slid down, easing the weight off her leg. I wonder if I'll ever find someone I could get so excited about, she thought. She'd dated a number of guys, but no one very seriously. She nearly always got asked to football games and dances, but she'd never had anyone steady. She'd never been in love.

She was glad Susan had a chance at that feeling. But as she walked into the kitchen and turned on the oven, Amy couldn't help wishing she'd find someone of her own.

Chapter
6

"Mom and I got everything for Marc's party yesterday, Dee." Kim opened her brown bag and set her apple and sandwich on the cafeteria table. She, Woody, and Dee had just joined the rest of the crowd.

"We're all set for a major pig-out, I can tell you," Woody chimed in. He patted his stomach happily.

"It won't be too much trouble to make those little pizzas?" Dee asked.

"Not a bit," Kim answered.

"I'll be there hovering over the bowls," Woody said smugly. "That's the deal we made. If I don't bother Kim and her mom while they cook, I get to taste what they're making."

"You're impossible," Kim said playfully and leaned over to give Woody a quick kiss on the cheek.

"What kind of cake are you making?" Holly turned to Dee.

"Chocolate with cherry filling," Dee said.

"M-m-m-m." Jeremy licked his lips as if he were about to devour a whole cake single-handedly. "That's the kind of cake you'd run after even if you had a broken leg."

"Speaking of broken legs, how are the wounds, Amy?" Woody asked.

"Okay," Amy laughed. "I'll be good as new in a couple days."

"She really hurt herself," Dee said, looking sympathetically across the table at her friend. "I was a witness, and that was some crash!"

"You'll be able to dance at Marc's party, won't you?" Elise asked.

"I'll give it a try!" Amy said.

"Which reminds me, I've got to make an announcement that came to me second-hand from Dee." Woody cleared his throat for dramatic effect. "Kim told me I made a mistake yesterday asking Marc what he was doing Saturday night. Dee doesn't want us to even *mention* Saturday to him. From now on, there's no such day in the week. Okay?"

"It's just if everybody asks him, he's going to start suspecting something," Dee put in, smiling at Woody. "Fiona and I had a pretty close call yesterday."

"No problem," Jeremy said.

"Mum's the word," Elise added, zipping an imaginary zipper across her lips.

"He doesn't know anything, Dee," Holly assured her. "You can just tell from how he's been acting."

"Where is he, anyway?" Woody asked.

"I haven't seen him," Dee said casually. She tried to keep from looking worried. She didn't want to act like anything was wrong, but the truth was she hadn't talked to Marc since yesterday afternoon when they'd had that fight-that-wasn't-really-a-fight.

After dinner she'd gone with her mother to the mall to get napkins and paper plates for Marc's party. When she got home she'd hoped there'd be a message waiting, but her little brother told her Marc hadn't called. After the way he'd acted that afternoon, Dee wasn't all that surprised. Still, not hearing from him bothered her.

For a while she considered calling him herself. Then she decided to let their problems go for another day. She was behind in her homework and needed time to catch up. And anyway, she didn't feel like a confrontation. If she got emotional, she might give away the secret about the party.

"It's just as well Marc's not around," Holly observed. "This way we can talk about his birthday."

"But speak of the devil." Woody pointed toward the cafeteria line. "Look who's over there with Bart and Ben."

"Let's talk about something else, quick!" Dee said.

"Let me tell you about the mating habits of the humming bird," Woody started out, and everyone at the table burst out laughing. "See, they fly through the sky. Zooooom!" Woody waved his arms excitedly.

"Okay, Woody," Kim said gently. "We've got it."

The gang watched Marc and the other boys walk toward them. Ben and Bart were smiling, but Marc looked serious. In fact, he didn't seem very excited to see his friends.

Dee especially was keeping an eye on Marc, and it seemed more obvious than ever to her that something must really be bothering him. She wanted to talk to him, but she dreaded it, too, especially since they hadn't gotten in touch last night. Is he going to sit down and act like nothing's wrong, she wondered. Will he say anything about missing her last night?

Dee smiled at Marc and waited for him to come and sit in the empty chair beside her, as he always did.

But when Marc walked up, he didn't even glance at her. He strode purposefully to the opposite end of the table, setting his tray down with a clatter.

Dee's face fell in surprise and disappointment. Having Marc get mad at her yesterday was bad enough, but having him ignore her completely was the worst thing she could imagine. Obviously something was seriously wrong between them. Dee's hands suddenly went cold as ice. If there hadn't been so many other people around, she probably would have burst into tears, but instead she took a long sip on the straw in her apple juice, hoping the gesture hid the sudden trembling of her lips.

As Marc calmly picked up his fork and started in on his enchilada, Dee tried even harder not to show that she was upset. There was no way she was going to let him know that his behavior was bothering her. If he chose to snub her without offering an explanation, then he deserved a little of the same treatment.

Fortunately, no one else seemed to notice that there was any tension between them. They all joked and laughed as usual and Dee pretended to get into the lunch-hour spirit.

Bart sat down in the empty chair next to Dee and gave a kiss on the nose to Holly, who was on his other side. Ben grabbed a chair from another table and moved it into the group so he could be next to Elise.

"Great stuff," Woody said sarcastically as he eyed the enchiladas the three boys had gotten in the cafeteria line.

"They wouldn't dare serve these south of the border," Bart agreed. "But when you're starved, you're starved."

"I just got a summer job at the El Toro restaurant," Elise said.

"Waitressing?" Amy asked.

"No, working at the cash register. My dad knows the owner and he said he'd hire me."

Woody shoved his hand across the table to shake Elise's. "Congratulations," he said. "With experience like that, you'll be able to face the enchiladas here at school next year without blinking an eye."

"You'll be eating dorm food," Jeremy reminded him. "That's no better."

"True," Woody admitted. "But then, the Barries will still be feeding me when I come home on vacations. They've got the best food in town."

"Agreed," Jeremy said.

"I'm looking for a job," Diana put in, leaning against him. Jeremy put his arm around her.

"What kind?" Holly asked.

"Anything but modeling." Diana giggled and gave Jeremy a knowing glance. Since the fiasco over the modeling job he'd gotten her not long ago, they'd had an understanding.

"Mom said kids our age are going to be out of work everywhere this summer," Amy said.

"We should get together and open some kind of business ourselves," Bart suggested. "Then we all wouldn't have to go to the trouble of looking for jobs."

"The Red and Gold Lawn Trimmers," Woody ad libbed. "Kennedy High Car Washers." He snapped his fingers. "I've got it! We could share a job as a life guard and each work just a half hour a day!"

A round of groans mixed with laughter came from almost everyone at the table. Dee didn't feel much like joining in. She stole a glance at Marc. He wasn't laughing, either. He was sitting kind of detached, buttering his roll as if that was the only thing he cared about in the world. Dee quickly looked back at her sandwich.

Marc hadn't said a word to anyone since he sat down, and Dee had clammed up, too. How could she talk when the boy she loved was acting like she didn't exist? Dee put a palm to her forehead. Her head had started to ache, and no matter how she tried to ignore it, she knew the pain came from feeling so hurt by Marc.

Dee took a bite of her sandwich and chewed it slowly. The ham and cheese suddenly tasted like cardboard. She put the sandwich back in its plastic bag and wadded up her napkin feeling as if she'd never enjoy lunch in the cafeteria with the gang again.

Amy's chair scraped against the linoleum floor as she stood up across the table from Dee. "I've got to study for my chemistry test," she announced. "There's still fifteen minutes before next class."

Marc glanced at Dee, then also stood up. "I've got the same test," he said turning to Amy. "I'll go with you."

Dee looked at Amy and their eyes met. Dee knew everyone at the table probably could read the hurt on her face, but she couldn't hide it. Amy gave her a sympathetic look and then waved good-bye to the group and headed for the door. Marc followed her.

Dee was still staring in disbelief as Marc stopped to put his tray through the kitchen window and then disappeared into the hall. How can this be happening, she wondered. Especially now of all times — right before the party. Thinking of all the planning, all the time, all the trouble she'd gone through made Dee's headache double its dull throbbing.

But there *must* be an explanation, she decided. Everything has one. The important thing now was to find out what it was.

Amy and Marc walked together in silence for a minute. She hadn't been able to help noticing what had just taken place — or rather what hadn't — between Marc and Dee. She was concerned and curious enough to just come right out and ask Marc about it. Dee was one of her best friends and she hoped maybe she could help somehow.

"Is anything wrong?" she asked as they turned down a corridor and headed toward the library.

"Wrong?" Marc raised his dark eyebrows.

"It seems like something's going on between you and Dee," Amy explained.

"Why do you think that?"

"Well, because you didn't sit by her. You ignored her completely," she said, surprised at the carefully neutral tone of his voice.

Marc's jaw tightened slightly. "There's nothing wrong, Amy," he said, dismissing her question.

"Then why — "

"Have you studied much for the chemistry test?" he interrupted.

Amy stared at him, completely puzzled. If she didn't know better, she'd think that the boy with the determined look on his face standing in front of her wasn't Marc at all. Marc was different — Dee was always the most important thing on *his* mind. He'd obviously just changed the subject on purpose, but Amy couldn't decide if she should let it drop or try to get him to talk about how he felt.

If I push him, he'll probably just get defensive, though, she thought. And that wouldn't do any good. They only had a few minutes before the next period anyway.

"I studied a lot yesterday," Amy said finally, figuring that ignoring Marc's behavior was best for now. "But there are a few more things I wanted to try and cram into my brain before class."

Without saying another word, she and Marc entered the library. The silence made Amy feel awkward, but making small talk didn't feel right, either.

She and Marc sat down at a library table together and each took out their chemistry books. They started reading through their notes as if they didn't even know each other.

Chapter
7

"Hey, Amy!"

When Amy heard her name above the noise in the hall, she turned on her heel, her long blonde hair swinging. Colin Edwards was waving at her. As she waited for him to catch up to her, she could see why Susan found him so attractive. He strode toward her, tall and handsome. A tousled lock of blond hair fell appealingly over his forehead and his smile was warm enough to melt butter.

"I see you're not limping so much today," Colin said.

"The leg's better." Amy's smile showed that she really appreciated his concern.

Colin started walking down the crowded hall with her toward their chemistry class. "Ready for the test?" he asked.

"Ready as I'll ever be!"

"It shouldn't be too hard."

"I hope not."

When they got to their classroom, Amy saw Marc already sitting at his desk, his head bent over his notes in a last-minute attempt to cram. She wished Colin good luck and took her regular place in the front row. He walked to the back and sat down.

For the next hour the only noises in the room were the scratching of pencils across paper and the soft rattling of the venetian blinds as a breeze blew through the windows. Amy concentrated on the test with the intensity of a surgeon in the operating room.

The problems seemed a little hard, but taking tests had always been easy for Amy. She wasn't conceited about it, but because she always studied so carefully, she actually enjoyed showing the teacher how much she knew. As she worked away at her desk, she felt pretty confident that Mr. Jessup would be pleased with the results.

Without even looking at her watch, Amy could tell when the hour ended. Students around her grew more restless, shuffled their feet, and shifted their chairs. Amy finished her test. When the bell rang, she quickly glanced back over her answers and folded her paper.

"Thanks," Mr. Jessup said with a smile as she handed it to him. "Did you have time to finish all the problems?"

"Yes," Amy said, smiling back. "Just barely."

Out of the corner of her eye, she saw Marc dash out the classroom door. Amy had figured he wouldn't wait to talk to her about the test. He might be afraid she'd bring up Dee again and make him feel awkward. But she wasn't about to pry.

Amy grabbed her books and went out into the hall. It would feel great to get home and relax awhile, she thought, especially after the test.

As Amy pictured the lemonade she'd make and the deck chair she'd sit on in her back yard, she felt a nudge at her elbow. She looked up and found Colin smiling down at her. Amy's day-dreaming eyes met his laughing ones.

"Hey, come back to earth," he said. "You look a few miles away."

"I'm a space cadet after a test." Amy smiled.

"I know what you mean. Do you think you did okay?"

"Hope so. How about you?"

Colin grinned. "Actually, I hate to say it but I think I aced it."

"That's because you like chemistry."

He nodded. "The way we wish Susan would like algebra," he said with a wink.

"You've got it." Colin would be surprised if he knew how interested in algebra Susan *was* these days, though, Amy thought. All Susan talked about — besides Colin — was equations, thanks to him.

"How's she doing, anyway?" Colin asked.

"Great. She was still up studying when I went to bed last night. And she talked about word problems at breakfast!" Amy shook her head.

"Nothing like $x = y$ with cornflakes."

She giggled. "At least she's studying," she said, taking an extra step to keep up with his long strides. "She's not all that crazy about school, as you may have gathered."

Colin wrinkled his forehead. "Not like you, huh?" he observed, his face a little more serious.

Amy shrugged. "Sisters aren't always alike," she pointed out.

"Yeah. Sometimes I think my brother's going to flunk out."

"I didn't know you had a brother."

Colin nodded. "Rich. He's a sophomore. A soccer and tennis freak. That's about all he cares about. It's sure not school."

"Sounds just like Susan," Amy said, smiling. "But Susan's smart," she added loyally. "She just doesn't try all that hard. I guess grades aren't everything."

"As long as she's not planning to be a math teacher." Colin grinned and pushed his glasses up higher on his nose. "That seems like it would be more your thing."

Amy shook her head decisively. "I might like to teach, but not math. Maybe biology. In a university, like Dad's. What about you?"

"I want to be an astronaut."

"Then *you'd* be the space cadet." She giggled.

"Right. Without even taking a chemistry test first!"

As Amy and Colin neared the exit to the parking lot, Amy turned to say good-bye.

"Good to see you," she said brightly. But Colin stopped her, putting a hand on her arm.

"Hey, wait," he said. "I'm going that way, too."

He pushed the door open for her, and they walked outside into the warm sunshine. Not a single cloud darkened the sky. White lilies bloomed in the flower bed beside the sidewalk. Amy breathed in the fresh air. Spring had definitely arrived.

"Great day, huh?" Colin tilted his head back to get the sunshine full on his face.

"Sure is," Amy agreed. She looked over at him and instead of looking quickly away again, her eyes lingered longer than she knew they should have. She couldn't help it — she was momentarily mesmerized. His blond hair shone in the light. The muscles ran smoothly across his shoulders.

Being with Colin on a day like this was really nice. Actually, Amy realized suddenly, being with him would be fantastic on any day at all.

She flashed him a smile and then tore her eyes away. She was feeling the same warm sensation she got when she lay out by the pool in the sunshine. The way his eyes crinkled up around the edges when he smiled back at her had made her take an extra breath.

But Amy couldn't very well forget Susan's excitement when Colin had left their house yesterday after the tutoring session. She couldn't start getting a crush on the same guy her sister wanted more than anything in the world.

With the same discipline that got her A's on tests, Amy shoved aside her feelings of attraction toward Colin. He'd never be more than a friend no matter how handsome he looked in the sunshine.

"Did you ride your bike to school?" she asked, trying to sound as casual as possible.

"It's over there." He pointed to one of the bike racks across the parking lot.

"Mine is, too," Amy said.

A few minutes later, they discovered their bikes had been leaning against each other all day, locked fender to fender.

"We probably just missed each other this morning," Colin said. "Looks like we're destined to ride home together, eh?"

They unlocked their bikes and pulled them out of the metal rack, then walked them slowly toward the street.

Colin stopped for a moment to adjust his backpack more securely. "Hey, Amy," he said casually. "Want to get an ice cream cone at Sticky Fingers?"

Amy looked at him in surprise. She tried to suppress the excitement that bubbled up inside her by swallowing hard. She was speechless. Rarely was she at a loss for words, but Colin had caught her completely off guard.

Part of her would rather get an ice cream cone with Colin than anything she could think of, but the other part knew she could never do it. No matter how attractive Colin was or how much she enjoyed being with him, if Susan found out, she'd be insanely jealous. Amy wouldn't dream of doing that to her.

"I can't." She spoke first and then tried to think of an explanation. "I mean, I'd really like to, but. . . ." She hesitated. "I've got to go to . . . the dentist for a checkup this afternoon!"

She felt her face grow warm and she was sure her cheeks were turning red. She'd never been any good at lying.

"Maybe another time." Colin sounded as if he were trying to make light of her refusal in spite of his disappointment.

"Sure," Amy said softly. But she knew she was lying again. She'd never be able to go out with Colin Edwards, even for something as simple as ice cream. He was Susan's, at least for now. And no matter how much Amy wished otherwise, there was nothing she could do about it.

"I've got to go to the mall anyway to get some sneakers," Colin said as he climbed onto his bike.

"Hope you find some good ones."

"Me, too. It could be a challenge with my giant feet." Colin grinned and held one of his feet up from the pedal. "The only good thing about them is there's no webbing between my toes."

Amy couldn't help laughing. "Duck feet are better than none at all."

"I've got barges."

As Amy started off down the street, Colin called back to her. "Good luck not having any cavities!"

Amy turned to wave to him and saw him grinning at her again. Obviously getting turned down for ice cream hadn't shaken his self-assurance. It didn't look like she had to worry about hurting his feelings.

It was her own feelings she had to worry about. To say she was torn was an understatement. How had she ever gotten into such a terrible, confusing situation?

By the time she got home and put her bike in the garage, Amy was even more agitated. But the minute she walked into the house she had to hide her feelings. Susan was waiting for her in the kitchen.

"Amy!" Susan greeted her excitedly. "I saw Colin at lunch."

"Good for you, Suze! How'd it go?"

"Great. We talked about my test on Friday. He said he was glad to hear I'm studying."

"I am, too. I know you'll do fine if you work at it."

"You know what?" Susan leaned her bare elbows on the kitchen counter and beamed at her sister.

"Hmmm."

"Miss Taylor called on me twice today, and both times I knew the answers!"

"Good for you!" Amy opened the refrigerator door. "If you get an A or B on your next test, I'll take you for an ice-cream cone. How's that?"

The minute Amy mentioned ice cream she regretted it. She stared blankly at the cans of soda and fruit juice in front of her. She knew she needed some time to be alone to think things over.

As she poured herself a glass of cranberry juice and grabbed a cookie, Susan began describing her conversation with Colin, obviously getting immense pleasure in relating each detail.

"He said he grows vegetables. I can show him some of your brussels sprouts and spinach, can't I?"

"Sure, Suze. I'm sure he'll be thrilled," Amy teased.

Underneath, though, she was more confused than ever. The fact that Colin was interested in gardening, too, drew her a little bit closer to him. She hurried for the kitchen door, eager to escape to her bedroom.

"Wait." Susan stopped her. "I want to ask you something."

"What?" Amy asked, slightly wary.

"Can I borrow your red T-shirt Monday? Not all day, just when Colin comes in the afternoon."

Amy gripped her cranberry juice glass so tightly she was surprised it didn't break. "Sure," she said, "any time." She ran up the stairs three at a time.

Chapter
8

Amy lay on her bed and stared out the window. The sky looked so blue and free and open. But inside Amy felt exactly the opposite.

She felt as if something were squeezing her, pressing down on her, locking her in on all sides.

She took a deep, shaky breath and leaned back further into her pale blue bolster. Closing her eyes, she could see Susan's face lighted up with excitement whenever she talked about Colin. Nothing could please Amy more than her sister's happiness. And now Colin was showing interest in *her*, instead of Susan.

For a moment Amy wondered if she'd done something to get herself into this impossible situation — encouraged Colin somehow. No, she decided in all fairness, she really hadn't. She guessed sometimes things just happened without anyone's intending them to work out in such complicated ways.

She opened her eyes again and her gaze fell on the brass unicorn paperweight Susan had given her for Christmas last year. It was one of Amy's most prized possessions, and she knew Susan had saved her allowance for weeks to buy it. She and Susan had always been close, more than ever in the past few months. Amy would never do anything to jeopardize that closeness.

Amy sat up and took a sip of cranberry juice. She flopped over on her stomach. The bedspread felt cool against her cheek. She tried to blot out her confusion by thinking of everything but Colin. Nothing helped. An image of him kept popping into her mind. She saw him wave good-bye to her all over again, his mouth turned up in that confident grin.

Why can't things be easier? she asked herself, hot tears springing to her eyes. Why can't I find someone to like that Susan's never even heard of?

The minute Amy asked herself that question, she sat up straight again. No matter how hard she tried to pretend she didn't like Colin, she had to admit that she did. And not just a little. A whole lot. There was no point denying it. She'd fallen for him just as hard as Susan had.

Amy sighed and slowly shook her head in dismay. Okay, so she liked Colin. There wasn't much she could do about that. But she could keep from acting on it. She had to let Susan have her chance first.

But what would she do if Susan ever found out Colin had invited her out? Amy didn't know how she could explain the situation to her sister without hurting her feelings. And what if Colin called her up at *home* and asked her out again? Susan would never forgive her.

Yet if Amy were honest with herself, she also knew she'd like nothing better than Colin's calling her. She imagined going out with him and it made her glow with warmth. They could go to a movie and get a pizza afterward. Colin could tell her more about his garden or why he wanted to be an astronaut. They could joke around together like they had this afternoon. He might hold her hand and later kiss her good-night. . . .

Amy shook her head as if she were telling someone "no," then realized she was actually saying "no" to herself. No, she couldn't go out with Colin if he asked her again. No, she shouldn't look forward to seeing him in chemistry class tomorrow. No, she had to keep herself from thinking about him. As hard as this situation was, she simply had to do right by her sister.

Amy rolled over on her side with a groan and shut her eyes again tightly. Every time Colin came to her mind, she tried to push him out of her thoughts. But it wasn't working.

Just as Amy began to get discouraged, she heard the phone ring. Susan's voice drifted up the stairs from the kitchen. "Amy, it's for you. It's Dee."

Slowly Amy pulled herself up from the bed and went out to the hall to answer.

"Hi, Amy," Dee said. "What're you doing?"

"Trying to recover from my chem test," Amy said. "I was going to call you in a while," she added, taking the phone into her room.

"I just got home." Dee paused a minute. "I guess there's no point in beating around the bush. What did you think about Marc at lunch?"

"I thought he was weird. I was amazed that you could sit there without showing how much he must have been bothering you!" Amy exclaimed.

"But you could tell he *was* bothering me?"

"Not from anything you did. But from how Marc was acting, you sure deserved to be upset," she said sympathetically.

"He really hurt my feelings," Dee said.

Amy sat down on her bed. "Did you talk to him last night like you said you would?"

"I was going to." Dee explained how Marc hadn't called when she'd been out and why she'd decided to let their problems go for another day. "I wish I'd phoned him," she added. "You were right about talking things through right when they're happening."

"To tell you the truth, I asked Marc what was going on when we were walking to the library," Amy said. "But he changed the subject."

"What'd you say?" Dee asked eagerly.

"Nothing much. I just asked if anything was wrong. I could tell he didn't want to talk."

"I just don't understand, Amy. I know when he gets mad at his brothers, he ignores them for a while. But he's never given me the silent treatment before." Amy could picture Dee shaking her head on the other end of the line. "It makes me so mad."

"I can't figure him out, either," Amy said in a soothing voice. "But you know, I had the feeling after lunch he felt kind of hurt, too. Like you."

72

"Hurt?"

"Mm-hmm. Like he was hiding something. But he'd never admit it. Not to me, anyway. You've really got to talk to him."

"I know," Dee agreed with a heavy sigh.

"Everything will just get worse if you don't. You have to call him — for the sake of the party if nothing else."

Amy thought it was strange for her to urge Dee to talk to Marc. Just in the last hour she'd gotten herself into a situation where she couldn't take her own advice. There was no way she could talk to Susan about what was happening with Colin. Being absolutely honest just wasn't possible in every circumstance.

For a moment both girls were silent, each lost in thought.

"You're right, Amy," Dee said finally. "I can't let Marc ruin everything."

"Good," Amy encouraged.

Dee sighed again. "Anyway, I still love the jerk." She laughed shakily.

When Amy didn't laugh along with her, Dee spoke again. "Amy, are you okay?"

Amy snapped out of her reverie. "What do you mean?"

"You seem a little out of it," Dee said.

Amy wished she could confide in her friend, but she couldn't say anything with Susan around.

"Hold on a minute," she said. Amy went into the hall and tiptoed down to the staircase landing to find out exactly where Susan was. Through the kitchen door, she saw her sister sitting at the table, her algebra book open in front of her. She wouldn't be able to hear what Amy said in her room.

Amy hurried back to the telephone. "Something lousy's happened, Dee," she whispered. "I can't talk about it now because Susan might come upstairs and hear me."

"Is it about her?"

"Partly."

"Do you want to go for a bike ride?"

"I can't." Amy pictured herself running into Colin. He'd know she'd lied about the dentist, and he'd probably think she hadn't wanted to go out with him.

"Why not?" Dee asked.

Amy opened her door a crack and looked out into the hall again to make sure Susan hadn't come upstairs. "Because I'm afraid of seeing someone," she whispered, closing the door gently. "It's a long story."

"Why don't you come over?" Dee suggested. "Drive along the side streets so nobody sees you. Wear dark glasses and a scarf over your hair. We could talk."

Amy thought quickly about sneaking to Dee's. Susan had said Colin lived on Maple Avenue. If Amy went a block the other way up Madison and turned left, she could get to the private lane behind Dee's house. No one would see her there. She wanted to talk to Dee so badly that the risk seemed worth it.

"Okay," she said finally. "I'll be there as soon as I can."

After she hung up the phone, Amy dashed to

her dresser. She had to laugh at herself as she took a bandanna out of her top drawer and tied it over her hair. It wasn't exactly a disguise, but with sunglasses maybe she wouldn't be recognizable, at a distance at least.

When she started out on her bicycle, she hardly noticed the slight stiffness in her leg because she was so busy looking around for Colin. But once she got to the private lane, she relaxed. Only about three people used it on any given day, and it ended right at the back of Dee's house. If she bumped into him on her way home, she could tell him she was coming back from the dentist.

Amy smiled with relief when Dee answered the back door and let her in after bursting out laughing at her costume. A few minutes later, the two girls sat cross-legged on Dee's bedroom floor, leaning against a pile of lavender overstuffed pillows and sipping peppermint tea.

Dee blew gently at the steam curling out of her cup. "This should calm you down a little," she said. "You look like you could use it as much as me."

"I can," Amy said with a sigh.

"So what's wrong?" Dee asked and leaned forward attentively to hear Amy's problem.

"It's Colin."

"Has he done something to Susan?"

"No. He hasn't done anything . . . exactly." As Amy began her tale, she felt confused all over again. This was going to be harder to talk about than she'd expected.

"What's the matter then?"

"I like him. That's what's the matter." Amy took a sip of tea, feeling a little like a criminal. "And obviously Susan does, too."

Dee nodded, her eyes widening in understanding. "Oh, I *see*."

"He asked me out this afternoon, Dee. He wanted me to get *ice cream* with him!" Amy said this as if Colin had asked her to elope with him.

"You turned him down?"

"I had to. If Susan found out, she'd never speak to me again."

"She'd get over it," Dee offered.

"No. I don't think so. Since Susan met Colin, she's finally gotten back to her old self. She's been so sad since our parents split up."

Amy sank farther back into the pillows and wished she could disappear forever into the soft stuffing. Stiffly, she uncrossed her legs, then crossed them again.

"I'm so confused, Dee," she finally said. "I want Susan to be happy. I have to be loyal to her. But I really like Colin myself. I don't know what I'll do if he ever asks me out again."

"He probably will, Amy," Dee said.

Amy looked at her friend with big, unhappy eyes. "I want to be free to get to know him, Dee. I'd hate to lose my chance." She rubbed her forehead with her fingertips as if she were trying to erase the whole situation from her mind.

Dee's cat Lily padded softly into the room and brushed against Dee's knees. As she petted Lily, Dee looked thoughtful.

Suddenly she snapped her fingers. "I've got it!"

she said, grinning. "I've got the perfect plan!"

"What's that?"

"Colin has a younger brother, Rich. Do you know him?"

Amy shook her head.

"Well, he looks like a younger version of Colin *and* he's Susan's age. Actually, he's got a lot in common with Susan." Dee presented this last fact in a significant tone.

"That's what Colin said," Amy agreed.

"Marc knows Rich from soccer." Dee's eyes sparkled triumphantly. "He could fix them up! Susan would be crazy about him. Then *you* could go out with Colin!"

The idea sounded too good to be true, but Amy forced herself to be realistic. Susan might not fall for Rich, and if Colin figured out something like this was going on behind his back, he might really be turned off. Not to mention the fact that Dee and Marc weren't even getting along.

"No offense, Dee, but how could you get Marc to help us if you two aren't even speaking to each other?" Amy asked.

Dee frowned. "I'm going to call him, don't worry. Maybe we can get together tonight and talk things through. I'll ask him about Rich and Susan then."

"Do you think he'll go along with the idea?"

"Sure," Dee said. "Even if he's mad at *me*, I know he'd always be glad to do you a favor. You know what else I'll do, I'll call Colin tonight and invite him to Marc's party," Dee added. "You can start getting to know him better then."

Amy folded her arms excitedly. "I wish this would all work out!" she said. Amy started to have some hope that both she and Susan could be happy — and still stay friends.

Chapter 9

After dinner Dee sat on her bed with Lily and tried to gather up enough courage to call Marc. She glanced down at her phone. It was just sitting there, waiting to be used. Picking up the receiver and dialing should be no problem. Still, Dee hesitated.

Since Marc had been so strange at lunch, she wasn't sure how he'd act if she called him. But she had no choice. Amy was right — Dee had to swallow her pride and talk to him — for the sake of the party if nothing else. She couldn't let all her arrangements for Saturday be ruined just because she and Marc were having problems. And really, the party was the least of it. She loved him and she missed him and that was reason enough to straighten things out.

Dee took a deep breath and reached for the phone. When Marc answered, she almost hung up again. Instead she swallowed, and gripped the receiver tightly.

"Hi, Marc," Dee said, knowing her voice was slightly distant, yet unable to control it.

"Dee," Marc said, surprised.

Dee gulped again. Just *say* it, she instructed herself silently. "Marc, I think we need to talk about some things."

"Like what?" he asked.

"Us." Dee's voice was small.

A silence spread over the line between them like a thin layer of fog.

"Okay," Marc said finally.

"Will you meet me at the sub shop in a while?" Dee asked. "It's hard talking on the phone."

"I have to help my mom with the dishes. How about in half an hour?"

"Seven-thirty?"

"Okay."

Dee put down the receiver and lay down on the bed to recover. Calling Marc hadn't been so bad. He'd been a little cool, but he'd agreed to meet her. He'd almost sounded like he wanted to. Dee began to feel more hopeful that maybe everything would work out in time for the party.

Quickly she got dressed in her new white jeans and a dusty pink oversized T-shirt. She stood in front of her mirror to brush her hair. She looked at herself critically and decided she looked good enough to meet what lay ahead with Marc.

Reaching for her straw purse, she started for the door. Just as she got to the hall, the phone rang.

"Can you come over?" Fiona asked. "Pam just called. Tonight's the only time she can help with the decorations."

Dee looked at her watch. Seven-ten. "I'm supposed to meet Marc at seven-thirty," she said.

"It'll only take a minute," Fiona urged. "At least we could get started on the sign. You and I could finish later."

Dee glanced down a little nervously at her watch again. If she stopped at Fiona's, she'd probably be late to meet Marc. Knowing he'd be waiting for her made her slightly uneasy.

But Fiona and Pam were being so helpful. If tonight were the only time all three of them could get together, then she'd have to go along with it. Marc wouldn't mind waiting a few minutes.

Dee told Fiona she'd be at her house as fast as she could.

"What do you think? 'Happy Birthday Marc'?" Dee giggled.

She and Pam and Fiona stood side by side on Fiona's porch, staring down at the long blank piece of paper.

"Can't get a better message than that," Pam teased, and shook her head.

"We can be original with the art work instead," Fiona suggested.

"How about a soccer team?" Pam bent down over the paper and made circles with her hands where the players could be drawn.

"That's too much like the way I'm decorating Marc's cake." Dee waved a hand dismissively.

"Why don't we just paint silly things. Anything that comes to our minds?"

"I've got it." Fiona grinned, her face lighting up with the beginnings of an idea. "We could draw a symbol for everyone at the party."

"I don't get it," Pam said.

"Woody could be a woodpecker with red suspenders. Kim could be a chocolate chip cookie. Dee could be a camera."

"That's a cute idea!" Dee clapped her hands. "Everybody would have to figure out what represented them on Saturday night."

"Great!" Pam nodded enthusiastically. "Marc can take the sign home for a souvenir afterward."

"Let's go to it," Fiona said. She rushed out of the room and brought back a fistful of pencils and erasers.

"Thanks." Dee took a pencil. "I sure appreciate you letting us do this here. I'd die if Marc came over to my house and saw the sign."

"Not much chance he'll find it here," Fiona said as she knelt down by the paper.

Dee couldn't help thinking that come to think of it there wasn't much chance Marc would have seen it at her house, either. He wasn't exactly beating her door down lately.

As the three girls started working, Pam held one end of the paper and Fiona the other while Dee blocked out "Happy Birthday, Marc!" in giant printed letters. Stooping over the paper with pencil in hand, she couldn't shake from her mind the image of Marc sitting in the sub shop waiting for her. If he were there already, he'd be drumming his fingers on the table and looking around for her.

Just thinking about it made her frown, but she kept on drawing. She and Pam and Fiona could get the sign started at least.

As she finished blocking in the "Marc," Pam and Fiona started drawing the symbols for their friends.

"I'm going to make a ballet slipper for you, Fiona," Pam said.

"I love it!" Fiona exclaimed.

"By the way, what color should the letters be?" Pam asked, turning to Dee.

"Marc's favorite color's red. Kind of like the color of a cardinal, I think," Dee informed her.

"We could mix some poster paint up now," Fiona offered. "Jeremy's got some."

Dee glanced at her watch for the umpteenth time: Seven-forty. Marc would be getting impatient by now.

"Could we do that right now, Fiona?" Dee asked. "I'm already late to meet Marc."

"Sure," Fiona said.

"If we decide on the color, then you and Pam could paint the letters or sketch a while. I could come back tomorrow and finish."

"You mix it," Pam said, looking up at them. "I want to finish Woody."

Dee bent down to study Pam's drawing and giggled. "He'll love that!"

"Does cardinal red have some blue in it?" Fiona called from the kitchen.

"Yeah." Dee rolled up her sleeves as she joined her.

The two girls sloshed paint around in a coffee can for a few minutes. Dee took a brush and dabbed a little color on a piece of notebook paper.

"A little more blue and we'll have it!" she declared.

Fiona poured in another drop of blue.

"Perfect!" Dee said.

"It's gorgeous," Fiona agreed. "Marc should really appreciate this personal touch."

"He will," Dee said. But the mention of his name was like an alarm clock going off inside her. She knew she had to hurry. "I've got to run," she said to Fiona. "We can mix more of this tomorrow if we need it."

Dee turned away from the sink abruptly. As she moved, she accidentally brushed against the coffee can of paint.

"Oh, no!" Fiona gasped. "Look at you!"

Dee glanced down at herself. A big red spot now decorated her T-shirt. "What am I going to do?" she said desperately. "How can I explain this to Marc?"

"Do you have time to stop at home and change?"

"I'm already late!"

"Come upstairs," Fiona offered. "I'll loan you something."

Dee followed Fiona to her bedroom. She stripped off her shirt and stood next to her friend while she rummaged through her closet practically dancing with impatience. Dee looked at her watch again. Seven-fifty-five. What if Marc got tired of waiting and left? That was too awful even to contemplate.

"Almost anything would go with those pants," Fiona said. "How about this?" She tossed Dee a light blue T-shirt with long sleeves and a scooped neck.

Dee wore a size larger than Fiona. The T-shirt might be a little snug. But as late as it was, Dee didn't have time to worry how the shirt fit.

"Thanks," she said, slipping into it as fast as she could.

She galloped back down to the porch to say good-bye to Pam, who was now sketching the woodpecker's suspenders. "I'm so late," Dee said breathlessly. "Thanks so much for helping."

"It's fun!" Pam said. "I'll start a horse for Diana when I finish this."

"Great!" Dee said. "Don't work too hard. I can finish up later."

She thanked Fiona and hurried outside. As she sped off to the sub shop in her mother's car, she glanced in the rearview mirror. All she'd need now was a speeding ticket, but the coast was clear.

She parked her car and ran across the sub shop parking lot to the door so quickly she almost barreled over someone who was leaving.

The minute she saw Marc, she knew he was really peeved. His forehead was rumpled into a first-class frown, which graduated to an A-number-one scowl when she got to his booth.

"Where have you been?" he asked, his eyes narrowed. "I've been waiting nearly an hour!"

"I'm sorry, Marc," Dee said sincerely. She

slid into the booth across from him and immediately noticed the Coke he'd ordered for her. Most of the ice had already melted.

"I had to stop at Sasha's to talk about a photo for the paper," she said. "It took longer than I thought."

Marc's scowl deepened. "You could have called," he said.

"I'm sorry, Marc," she repeated. "I couldn't help being late."

Marc crossed his arms over his chest. "Yeah. The good old *Red and Gold*. I guess you've got your priorities."

Looking across the table at him, Dee found herself starting to feel more than just hurt. She was getting mad. For weeks she'd been working so hard to get Marc's party organized, working hard because he was her boyfriend, and she wanted this to be his best birthday ever. And the way he was acting these days wasn't helping any. Even if he didn't know about her plans, it wasn't like him to be so unreasonable.

But when she thought about the situation, she could see his side, tonight at least. She didn't like to be kept waiting, either, especially all alone in a restaurant.

Quickly Dee decided to let Marc's grumpiness go for the moment. Maybe if she started talking about Amy and Colin first, she could warm him up a little before she confronted him with their own problems.

"I wanted to ask if you'd do something for me," she began. "Amy's having some trouble, and I think maybe we can help."

86

"How?" Marc asked, his face still rigid.

Dee explained the situation between Amy and Susan and Colin. "When she came over today after he'd asked her out, she was really upset. I've never seen her get such a bad crush on a guy."

Marc's face reddened as he listened. "So what am *I* supposed to do?"

Dee could tell Marc was holding something back. He looked as if he might explode, in fact. "You could fix up Susan with Rich Edwards," she said, trying to ignore his discomfort and go on with her plan. "I'm sure they'd hit it off. Then Amy could date Colin."

Marc didn't take his eyes off her. Dee noticed his jaw clench the way it did when he played badly in a soccer game and started to get mad.

"Marc, what's the matter?" she asked finally, no longer able to pretend everything was all right.

"What's the matter?" he said, shaking his head in disbelief. "I'll tell you. What's the matter is that I don't see how you find time to be meddling in everyone's life when you have so little time for me."

Dee stared at him, too shocked to speak.

"When *I* asked you to go for a Coke yesterday, you couldn't," Marc continued. "But as you just told me, when Amy called you up a little later, you went for a bike ride with her."

"She didn't call me," Dee blurted out. "I called her."

"That's even worse. Why didn't you call *me*?"

Suddenly Dee felt completely flustered. She

couldn't tell Marc she'd called Amy just to talk about him. She couldn't say she'd refused to be with him yesterday because she had to get ready for his birthday party. She'd been trying so hard to make everything work, and he was making it impossible.

"I had photos to develop yesterday," she began defensively.

"Sure. I've heard that before," Marc said sarcastically as he leaned toward her. "All you ever do is develop photos. Half your life goes to *The Red and the Gold*. I'm sick of it, Dee." He banged the table with his fist. "Spring soccer training's almost over. Are we ever going to have time for each other? Or are you just going to move in at the newspaper?"

Dee's hand curled involuntarily into a fist. "Of course I'm not moving in at the paper," she said sharply. "That was really a dumb thing to say."

Marc wadded his straw wrapper into a tiny ball and threw it on the table. "Sometimes I think you'd rather be dating *The Red and the Gold* than me," he exclaimed. "You've been so wrapped up in your work you don't even see what's going on around you."

Angry tears slid down Dee's cheeks. She was even more at a loss for words than before. Of course she'd been wrapped up in other things lately: busy planning the party for *him*!

Sure, *The Red and the Gold* took a lot of time, especially with all the spring activities the last few months. But Dee had spent lots of time with Marc. He didn't have any right to complain.

Dee reached for a napkin and took a swipe at her tears. Splotches of mascara came off on the paper. "You're being really mean, Marc," she said. "And you were horrible at lunch today." She dabbed at her eyes again. "I don't know what's wrong with you. I've been spending plenty of time with you. You shouldn't be criticizing me."

"*You* may think you're spending time with me, but I don't," Marc said. "And I'm half of us. Or I thought I was."

"What do you want? A clinging vine who follows you around all the time and doesn't have any interests of her own?" Dee asked, her voice a little shaky because she was still on the verge of tears.

"No, I don't want that." Dee had never seen him look so mad before. His cheeks were as flushed as hers.

"Never mind," he said finally. "You obviously don't understand. I don't see any reason to sit here and try to get through to you."

"All right then," Dee said.

She yanked at her purse strap and pushed herself out of the booth. Just as she was about to leave, she whirled around to face Marc again. Her world might be falling apart, but maybe she could salvage her friend's. "Even if *we're* not getting along, will you fix up Rich and Susan?" she asked icily. "I promised Amy we'd try."

"Okay," Marc said through gritted teeth.

Tears started down Dee's face again as she hurried toward the sub shop door.

Chapter
10

The minute Amy walked through the door of her chemistry class, she automatically looked toward the back of the room for Colin. She wasn't disappointed. He waved and smiled at her while she sat down at her desk in the front row.

All through class, Amy tried to pay attention to Mr. Jessup's lecture, but her mind kept drifting to thoughts of Colin, just seven rows behind her. Feeling he was staring at her didn't exactly help her concentrate. Halfway through class, Amy brushed her hand over the back of her neck, where she felt prickles from what she thought was Colin's gaze. Without even being able to see him, Amy was as drawn to him as iron to a magnet.

Soon after Mr. Jessup handed back their tests and talked briefly about the answers, the bell rang, and Amy suddenly found herself in as much conflict as she'd felt after class the day before. She really wanted to see Colin again. She'd been waiting to see him excitedly all day, in fact. And yet she wondered if she shouldn't sprint for the door. Maybe it would be better to avoid him altogether.

In a way, Amy was afraid to see him for fear he'd suggest they do something together. If she turned him down twice, he'd probably never bother with her again. But she couldn't agree to go out with him until she knew if Dee's plan for Rich and Susan had worked. Days might pass before she'd know for sure.

Amy sat at her desk for a moment and tried to collect her thoughts. To stall for time, she shuffled through her papers and pretended to look over her test again. She could always keep from bumping into Colin in the hall by staying late to talk to Mr. Jessup about one of the problems.

Still trying to decide what to do, Amy raised her head cautiously and glanced around the room. To her surprise, Colin was standing at the end of her row. Obviously he was waiting for her. As she smiled at him, her heart beat just a bit faster. He smiled back, and his blue eyes shone behind his glasses. Amy felt her cheeks turn pink.

Knowing she couldn't avoid him now, she quickly collected her books and stood up to meet him. Together she and Colin walked outside into the hall.

"How'd you do on the test?" he asked.

"I got an A. What about you?"

"The same. I knew it was easy."

Amy nodded agreement. "It's good to get the test back and know for sure, though."

"Right," Colin said.

In the crowded hall, he walked along beside Amy especially close. Their arms brushed sometimes when a large group of students passed by in the other direction. Amy was more aware than she wanted to be of even his slightest touch.

"Did everything go okay at the dentist?" Colin asked, looking down at her.

For a moment she forgot about her excuse and looked back at him blankly. "Um . . . yeah!" she said, blushing again from lying. "No cavities."

"That's good." Colin smiled. "Just be glad you don't have braces."

"You did, huh?"

"Till last year. *Not* a pretty picture." Colin clacked his teeth together, making a silly face.

Amy giggled and pretended to peer at his teeth as he smiled. "Looks like it was worth it," she observed.

"I guess so. It wasn't too bad. Except for the time my top braces locked to my bottom ones and I couldn't eat or even talk for a week."

"No, really?" exclaimed Amy, and then she saw his eyes twinkling mischievously. "Oh, you're bad!" She gave his arm a playful push. They both laughed heartily.

"So, how's Susan doing?" Colin asked. "Is she still studying hard?"

"Like crazy," Amy said. "I mean, if she doesn't get an A tomorrow, no one will."

"I hope she does. It'd be grim if she flunked the whole semester. She's just got two weeks to turn the F around."

"I think she will." Amy smiled affectionately.

"When she makes up her mind about something, nothing can stop her."

"We'll know when she gets the test back Monday," Colin said thoughtfully.

Amy studied the expression on his face as he talked about her sister. For a moment, she wondered if maybe Colin liked Susan — more than just as her tutor and friend. He always asked about her and seemed interested in her studying. But Amy pushed the thought away. He'd invited *her* out, hadn't he?

As she and Colin reached the door to the parking lot, Colin stopped for a moment and brushed his hand across her shoulder. Amy felt a trail of warmth across her skin underneath her thin cotton sweater.

"I've got to get to a Computer Club meeting," he said. "Back down the hall in Miss Taylor's room."

Just then Amy realized he'd walked out of his way to see her to the door. She lowered her eyes and smiled with pleasure.

"Have fun at the meeting," she said, looking up again.

"Oh, I will." Colin turned to go, but not until he'd held her gaze for a long, electric moment. "See you tomorrow," he called back to her as he started back the way they'd come.

Amy walked outside to her bike in a dreamy daze. She was relieved Colin hadn't asked her out again, and yet she was disappointed. She was excited about the way he'd looked at her when he said "See you tomorrow," but it was a little unsettling, too. She wondered if the situation would ever be resolved. It was all up to Susan and Rich.

That evening Amy sat at her desk, her head bent over her history book. But her mind wasn't exactly on the causes of World War II.

She shifted her weight in her chair and pushed her elbows against her desk top. Then she reached down to pet Sam, who lay at her feet. Looking outside into the dark, balmy night, she heard a few crickets chirping on the lawn and wished summer would hurry and arrive. Studying was hard in this warm weather, especially now that Colin was distracting her.

Except for a quick conversation in the cafeteria at lunch, Amy hadn't had a chance to talk to Dee all day. And since the crowd had been sitting there, she hadn't asked about how things went with Marc or if Dee had been able to talk to him about fixing up Rich and Susan. Marc hadn't even shown up at the table for lunch. Amy hoped his absence didn't mean more trouble for Dee.

She tried to force her thoughts back to World War II. She ran her hand over the globe on her desk and looked to see just where Berlin was. But she knew she was just procrastinating. What she really wanted to think about was Colin.

She wondered what he was doing just then. He was probably working at his desk, like her. What if he was thinking about her, too? The idea sent a tiny snap of excitement up her spine.

As Amy shifted positions in her chair again,

the telephone rang. She jumped to answer it.

"Amy?" Marc asked. "I need to talk to Susan . . . about Rich Edwards."

Amy gulped, then felt a thrill that left her slightly tingly. Obviously Dee and Marc had talked about Dee's plan. Amy wished she could thank Marc for his help now, but she couldn't risk saying anything Susan might overhear.

"Just a minute, Marc," she said.

Amy called her sister, then went back to her room. But she left her door open just a crack to hear the conversation.

"Hi, Marc," Susan said. "How you doing?"

Amy would have given anything to hear Marc's end of the conversation.

After a few seconds Susan spoke again. "No, I don't know him."

To Amy, the next few minutes dragged more slowly than waiting for Christmas. She strained to listen, turning around at her desk and looking into the hall. All she saw was Susan's back.

Finally Susan said, "That really nice of you, Marc. I'd like to, but I can't."

Amy closed her eyes and put her head in her hands. A wave of disappointment washed over her.

"I've already got other plans," Susan continued.

Amy could hardly believe what she was hearing. Dee's scheme wasn't working. Susan was messing everything up. Amy looked out the window again but the night no longer seemed warm and inviting. It looked pretty dark to her now.

She heard Susan hang up the phone and push her door all the way open.

"Amy?" Susan said.

"Hum?" Amy replied, still staring out into the darkness.

"Get this — Marc wanted to fix me up with Colin's *brother* Dick. Or was it Rick? Something like that. Can you imagine such a crazy coincidence?"

"Sounds good to me," Amy said halfheartedly.

"Not to me," Susan said with determination. "If I can't go out with Colin, I don't want to be with anybody."

"Maybe his brother's cute," Amy said reasonably.

"I don't care. It wouldn't be the same."

"You'd never know till you met him," Amy argued, but she knew trying to get Susan to change her mind was useless. She had to be careful anyway. If she got too pushy, Susan might suspect something. It was definitely a no-win situation.

Susan plopped down on Amy's bed. "I saw Colin after school this afternoon," she said, her face dreamy. "He was on his way to a Computer Club meeting."

Susan must have just missed seeing her with Colin, Amy realized. What a close call.

"He asked me if I'd been studying," Susan continued. "I told him I was going to get an A-plus on my test tomorrow."

"He must have been psyched," Amy said, suddenly feeling tired.

"He seemed happy about it. I'm going to show Colin I'm smart if it's the last thing I do."

Susan jumped up from Amy's bed with a

bounce. "You know what I've been thinking?" she said as she headed toward the door.

"No, what?"

"About inviting him to Casey Simmon's swimming party. Two weeks from now. Do you think he'd go?"

"I don't know, Susan," Amy said honestly. "I really don't know."

Chapter
11

When Dee heard the phone ring, she got even more tense than she'd been all day — if that were even possible, she thought wryly. If it was Marc she had no idea what she'd say to him.

Today had been just about the worst day she'd had since falling down at the cheerleader tryouts last fall. After her fight with Marc last night, she'd hardly slept. When she got to school, she was exhausted. All morning she dragged from class to class like a weary robot, hoping she'd see Marc, but also hoping she could avoid him. When he never showed up in the cafeteria at lunchtime, she felt hurt all over again — and angry, too.

Even after a day like this, though, Dee kept telling herself the situation wasn't hopeless. Couples had misunderstandings all the time and worked them out. She and Marc were no exception.

But still Dee hated having problems with Marc

at all, worrying that they might be in real danger of breaking up. The timing was the worst of all. Why did she and Marc have to have their first real fight just before his birthday?

The phone kept ringing, and Dee waited for her little brother Billy to answer it. She dreaded hearing the call was for her and that it was Marc — and at the same time she thought she'd die if it wasn't.

"It's for you, Dee," Billy shouted up the stairs.

"Thanks," Dee called back. Her heart jitter-bugged as she lifted the phone.

It was Marc. After a curt hello, he launched into a speech with the tone of a salesman about to close a deal. "I just talked to Susan," he announced. "She can't go out with Rich. She has other plans."

"That's too bad," Dee said, forgetting herself for a moment as she imagined how disappointed Amy would be.

"Rich seemed pretty enthusiastic," Marc continued. "But it just wasn't meant to be."

"Could you try another time?" Dee asked.

"He probably wouldn't go for it. He wouldn't want to get turned down twice."

From the finality in Marc's voice Dee knew arguing with him would be useless. She was surprised that he'd even bothered to call at all. But he and Amy were good friends. Obviously he was doing all this for her, not Dee. Dee knew him too well not to realize that he was still mad about last night.

"I also wanted to tell you," Marc went on, then

paused as if he were trying to pick just the right words. "I can't come watch the movie with you Saturday night."

"You what?" Dee gasped.

"Mom and Dad want me to go see Grams in the hospital."

"But can't you go during the day?"

"No. The soccer game, remember?"

Of course, Dee remembered. But she couldn't believe what Marc was saying. She tried to keep from panicking.

What did he mean he couldn't come over? The whole crowd would be waiting to surprise him! Dee had already paid the deposit for the food and worked out all the decorations and entertainment, to say nothing of going with Dick Westergard to buy Marc's calculator just this afternoon. How could he possibly be telling her now he wasn't coming?

"I remember the soccer game. And I'm sorry your grandmother's sick," Dee said, trying to keep her voice from shaking and revealing how upset she was. "But couldn't you visit her another time?"

"Mom wants me to go with them Saturday night," Marc insisted, his voice cold.

"Would she mind if you didn't?"

"She specifically asked me."

"But couldn't you go early Saturday morning *before* the game?"

"No, I — "

Dee didn't let him finish. "Look, I'll talk to you later," she burst out. If she listened to another word, she was likely to say something she'd really regret.

Dee slammed down the phone before Marc could get another word in. What difference did it make if the noise blasted his ear? If she'd talked to him any longer, she'd either scream or cry. Neither reaction would have been right. For now Dee had to calm down and figure out what to do. If she didn't do something quick, the party would be ruined.

She threw her sociology book angrily at her bed. Squeezing her hands into fists so tight her fingernails dug into her palms, she wished Marc were there just then so she could wring his neck.

Her head spinning, she stormed into her darkroom to be by herself and think. She'd never been faced with such an impossible situation before. And if she couldn't figure out what to do on her own, she'd have to go downstairs and tell her mother. That meant getting her upset, too.

Dee grabbed a few negatives of the track stars she'd photographed Monday. Holding them up to the light, she tried to decide which one to print first. But she could hardly keep her mind on what she was doing.

Marc's grandmother's been in the hospital for almost a month, she thought, her teeth clenched. He'd always gone to visit her on Saturday mornings, even when he *did* have a soccer game later in the day. And sometimes he *missed* games to see Grams — this was only a spring training session. He could do the same this weekend if he wanted to. He was just backing out of Saturday night because he was mad at her.

Dee felt so furious — and practically hysterical — that she couldn't concentrate. Her mind darted from one thing to another — an image of Marc calling Susan, the recipe she'd found for his cake, the red letters on the birthday sign she'd finished for him this afternoon.

Finally, she gave up trying to pick out the right negative. Any one would do. Without even looking at the one she chose, she lay it in her enlarger, but she couldn't see straight enough even to focus the lens. Dee knew she was too upset to work.

She turned off the enlarger light, slammed out of the darkroom, and stomped down the hall to her bedroom. After pacing up and down her room enough times to wear a path in the rug, she got herself under control enough to dial Amy's number.

"What am I going to do?" Dee moaned after relating the details of her conversation with Marc.

"I don't know, Dee," Amy said. "What's gotten into him, anyway?"

"He's angry. Whenever he's upset with his family, he gets quiet and works things out in his mind. I *guess* that's what he's doing now."

"But it's not fair to you!" Amy exclaimed.

"You're telling me," Dee said, running a hand roughly through her short hair.

"If he had any idea about the party, he wouldn't act like this," Amy said. "He wouldn't try to ruin everything just to get back at you. He's not like that."

"I know, I know. But I can't very well tell him what's going on and expect he'll suddenly cheer up for Saturday. If he's going to be such a jerk, I'm not sure I even want him here!"

"Oh, come on, Dee," Amy soothed. "You're just upset. You know you don't mean that."

"I mean it right now." And Dee knew she did. She'd tried all week to make things work with Marc. But no matter what she did, he still wouldn't meet her halfway. Dee didn't think she deserved such bad treatment just because Marc wanted her to spend more time with him. He was being completely unreasonable.

"Well, what *are* you going to do?" Amy asked, bringing the conversation back to their central dilemma.

"I don't know. This is the worst jam I've ever gotten into." Dee threw herself onto the bed, phone in hand.

"You're probably right," Amy agreed. "But you have to figure something out."

"What, though?"

"Have you talked to your mom?"

"No. She has no idea what's going on. If she knew how Marc was acting, she'd just get upset, too."

"She might have some good advice, though."

"She'd just tell me to do whatever makes me happy." Dee said. "And that would be absolutely no help at all."

"Do you want to call the party off?" Amy asked quietly.

"I don't know." Dee groaned and pressed her forehead with her palm. "It seems like such a waste. It's all ready and I'd be letting everybody down."

"Then go ahead and have the party. If you can get Marc to show up, fine. If he doesn't, we can get together anyway. Have an Easter celebration or something!"

"Yeah," Dee said bitterly. "With a cake that says, 'Happy Birthday Marc.' "

"Everybody's going to know Marc backed out anyway," Amy pointed out. "What the cake says doesn't matter."

"It just makes me mad," Dee said.

"I know. . . ." Amy paused. "I know."

Dee sat and tried to think for a moment. Amy was right. Canceling Marc's party would be dumb, even if Marc didn't show up. All her efforts — to say nothing of her mother's and her friends' — would go to waste. The crowd would find out about her and Marc's problems sooner or later. It might as well be sooner.

At least Dee could take comfort in knowing that some day Marc would find out what a jerk he'd been. He'd be sorry then.

"Okay, Amy," Dee said finally with a sigh of resignation. "The party's on. Marc can go visit his grandmother for the rest of his life for all I care."

"Great!" Amy said. "Maybe tomorrow I can talk to him and get him to come anyway."

"Don't hold your breath."

"I won't. But I'll give it a try. I'll track him down after chemistry and persuade him."

"I almost forgot!" Dee exclaimed. "I know you can't talk about this with Susan there, but Marc said he called her about Rich."

"Yeah?" Amy said in a neutral tone. It sounded to Dee as if Susan must be within hearing range.

"He said Susan wouldn't go out with Rich," she added.

"Right. I know," Amy's voice was still blank.

"I'm really sorry, Amy."

"Yeah. Me, too."

"But Colin's coming to the party," Dee declared, certain *this* news would cheer up her friend. "I finally got hold of him."

"For all the difference that'll make," Amy said. This time her voice cracked a little.

"Don't worry. We'll figure something out," Dee assured her.

"I doubt it," Amy said, discouraged.

"Everything's so hard," Dee observed with a deep sigh.

"You're telling me!" her friend agreed.

After Dee hung up the phone, she went to bed without even finishing her homework, but she didn't fall asleep for a long time. She couldn't get Marc out of her mind.

Love really wasn't easy, she finally decided. Not in the beginning, not even after being a couple for months. All along the way from start to finish, it seemed like all love meant was solving problems.

Chapter
12

As Amy walked to chemistry, she peeked down the hall to see if Colin was coming along looking for her as he had before. She wanted so much to see him, even though she still felt the same nagging conflict. Knowing Dee's plans for Rich and Susan had bombed only made it worse. For a while Amy had been hopeful, but now her future with Colin had dimmed to nothing.

As she entered the classroom, she expected to meet his blue eyes smiling at her from the back row, but his desk was empty. She sat down, deflated. Colin must not be coming today for some reason, she thought. Was he sick? Would he miss Dee's party tomorrow night?

Amy's shoulders drooped slightly in disappointment. Well, maybe it's for the best, she told herself. If I don't see Colin this afternoon or at the party, I don't have to worry about betraying Susan.

Just as the tardy bell rang, Marc ran through the door. Mr. Jessup glanced up from where he was writing at the blackboard and frowned. Then, sitting on his desk at the front of the room, he began his lecture.

Out of the corner of her eye, Amy watched Marc sink down into his seat. He looked out of breath from running but he also looked miserable, as if he'd just lost his best friend.

Amy's heart gave a sympathetic throb. Marc really *was* losing his best friend. If he and Dee didn't get over this disagreement pretty quickly, they might very well break up. Someone simply *had* to get Marc to his birthday party, for Dee's sake and his own. They were both Amy's friends, people she cared a lot about. It looked like it was up to her to take some action.

Amy tried to keep her attention fixed on Mr. Jessup, but without Colin there to keep her attention perked, the class seemed to drag on interminably. Usually Amy loved chemistry, but the subject had lost some of its spark for her today. She missed the warmth and energy she'd felt the past few days, just knowing Colin was in the room.

When class was finally over, Amy jumped up from her seat to corner Marc before he could escape through the door and disappear in the crowded hall. But he'd been even quicker than she had. She had to chase him halfway down the math and science wing before she got close enough to shout at him.

"Marc! Hey, wait a minute!"

He turned around slowly. His usually sparkling

eyes were somber and listless. He waited for Amy to catch up without saying a word in greeting.

"You look kind of upset," Amy said, hoping she could get the subject out in the open right in the beginning.

"It's been a lousy day."

"How come?"

"Everything," Marc said evasively.

"I know how that is," Amy sympathized, then paused for a moment. "I talked to Dee last night," she went on boldly. "She was pretty upset, too."

"Yeah, I know." Marc said. He and Amy started down the hall together.

"I don't want to pry or anything," Amy continued, "but if I can help, I'd be glad to."

"Nothing can help," Marc said. His hands were shoved deep in his pockets and he kept his eyes glued to the floor as they walked along.

"You mean it's that hopeless?" Amy asked with a smile, trying to lighten up the conversation a little.

Marc didn't even try to smile back. "Dee's really mad. Things are pretty bad between us."

"She thinks you're mad at her, too," Amy admitted.

Marc's mouth tightened into a straight line. "I am."

"But you look more upset than mad," she observed gently.

"I just wish this whole mess had never started!" Marc burst out. He kicked angrily at a radiator, sending a clanging echo down the hallway.

"I bet Dee feels that way, too," Amy said encouragingly.

"I doubt it."

"Really," she urged. "I'm sure she's sorry, too."

Amy wished she could come right out and tell Marc just how sorry Dee was. Sure, Dee was hurt about their fight, and mad that the party might be spoiled, but if she and Marc broke up, Amy knew Dee would be terribly hurt.

"You know you still care about her, Marc." Amy was determined to get through to him without giving anything away about the party. "You're mad right now, but you don't want to break up. I can tell."

"I know," Marc admitted. His face looked even more glum.

"Dee said you broke your date tomorrow," Amy continued.

"Yeah."

"Why don't you call her back and tell her you'll come over after all? If you'd both quit acting so dumb and sit down and talk, you could clear everything up!" She grabbed Marc's arm and made him look at her.

"If I called her she'd probably hang up on me." Marc met her eyes unhappily. "She was really mad last night, Amy. I mean steaming."

"I don't know about that." Amy shook her head firmly. "I bet she'd be glad to hear from you."

"I'm not so sure."

"Then show up at her house and surprise her!" Amy suggested, smiling. "Once she sees you, she'll be happy you came over. I know she will!"

Marc still looked wary, but his eyes brightened

slightly. "Do you think so?" he asked hopefully.

"I *know* so."

"Well. . . ." Mark hesitated.

"Will you do it?" Amy urged.

"I guess," he said.

"Good!" Amy grinned at him and punched his arm playfully. "You promise? I can't stand seeing two people I care so much about mess everything up like this."

"Okay, okay." Marc grinned back. "Don't worry. I'll do it."

A minute later Marc turned toward the gym for soccer practice. This time he was the one to put a hand on Amy's arm. "Thanks," he said. "You're a good friend, Amy."

"Any time." She grinned at him again.

"And Amy . . ." Marc hesitated a moment. "I'm sorry Dee's plans for Susan and Rich didn't work. Dee told me what was going on with you and Colin. We'll figure something out."

"Thanks," Amy said lightly. "I appreciate it."

When Amy went outside to get her bike, she couldn't keep from smiling. Marc's concern about her and Colin made her feel more hopeful. And besides, she thought, it's not every day I get someone as stubborn as Marc to agree to go to his own surprise birthday party! Dee would be thrilled when she told her the news. Their lives were all looking up.

Amy located her bicycle and unlocked it. Just as she raised the kick stand, she heard someone calling her name. She turned around. Colin was jogging toward her across the grass, looking kind of like a professional athlete or maybe a movie star. Waving at him, Amy thought he was even more handsome than she remembered. Her palms grew a bit damp, and she wasn't sure if it was because of Colin or the warm afternoon sunshine.

"Hi, Colin!" she said when he got closer. "Missed you in class."

"How was it?" he asked cheerfully.

"The usual. Mr. Jessup talked a lot about an experiment we're supposed to do next week."

"I had to meet with the vice-principal about running for student government, and this was the only period he could schedule a meeting. Can I borrow your notes?"

"Sure."

Amy shrugged off her backpack and reached inside for her chemistry notebook. She stopped for a second, trying to remember if she'd doodled Colin's name in the margin of the paper or anything silly like that. No, she thought, not today at least.

Colin put Amy's notebook into his backpack. "Thanks a lot. I'll get these back to you Monday if that's okay."

"Fine," Amy said. "How did the meeting go? Who's running for president?"

"Ben Forrest. And maybe me."

"You're running?" Amy's eyes widened in surprise.

"I'm thinking about it." Colin shrugged sheepishly. "I figure I'm as capable as the next guy."

"I'll vote for you," Amy assured him, smiling.

"Thanks! That's one I can count on anyway."

Amy watched as Colin unlocked his bicycle

and pulled it out of its slot in the bike rack. He steered it a few steps toward her, stopped, and looked into her eyes. "Want to ride over by the river?" he asked. "It's such a nice day."

Amy gripped her handlebars. "I . . ." she began, then hesitated.

What could she possibly say? This terrible situation was happening all over again. Colin's invitation was what she'd been hoping for, and yet it was the worst thing that could happen — at least right now. Amy hadn't been expecting to see Colin this afternoon. She wasn't ready for this.

As she hunted desperately for something to say, an awkward silence spread between her and Colin, putting still more pressure on her to speak. "Thanks, Colin," she started again, then paused, swallowing hard.

If she went for a bike ride with Colin, Susan was bound to find out. Amy had no idea what she could tell her, or whether Susan would get really mad.

Suddenly, though, it occurred to Amy that she and Colin had a perfect right to be friends. Riding along by the river was no big deal. Their talking wouldn't mean anything serious, and it certainly shouldn't hurt Susan.

Amy smiled brightly at Colin. "Sure," she said. "A bike ride sounds fun!"

Colin swung his leg over his bicycle and settled down on the leather seat. "Let's go!"

As they started pedaling out of the parking lot toward the street Amy noticed how the wind swept through Colin's blond hair. She wondered if she would ever stop being so attracted to him.

Her heart beat a little faster — from the pleasure of Colin's company and from the physical exertion of riding her bike. Amy found herself completely absorbed in Colin's every move — the motion of his legs as he pedaled along in front of her, the click of the gears when he shifted, the way he leaned over low when they went downhill. Amy was so distracted she was surprised she didn't run off the road.

Colin motioned for Amy to turn a corner with him. "I want to show you something," he called back to her.

Amy followed him half a block down the next street until he pulled his bike over to the curb and stopped in front of a house.

"Look." He pointed. "That's going to be the world's greatest vegetable garden. Sure wish it were mine."

Amy saw a huge plot of ground, all dug up, the earth rich and dark. Row after row of seedlings had sprung up with tiny, tender shoots. Poles were already stuck into the ground for the beans. The tiny tomato plants were strung to stakes.

"I've been watching this for weeks," Colin confessed with a smile, his gaze sweeping the area, taking in every detail.

"It's going to be fantastic," Amy agreed.

"It makes my garden look like a flop!" he said, laughing.

"I haven't even had a chance to start mine."

"You're into gardening?" He looked at her with interest.

"I've helped my mother garden every year since I was six, and I've had my own for years."

"Me, too." Colin grinned.

"Since we just moved to our house, though, I haven't been able to work on one yet."

"I can give you a bunch of tomato seedlings," Colin offered.

"Great!" Amy said enthusiastically.

Colin pushed his bike off from the curb. "I'll bring them over when I see Susan on Monday," he said.

For just a moment Amy panicked. If Colin showed up with tomato plants, Susan would know Amy had been spending time with him. Would she be jealous? Well, she and Colin were just friends after all. Why shouldn't they share things?

Amy and Colin pedaled together over a small hill and then approached the river. In the distance the banks were lush with fresh spring grass. Greg Montgomery and his crew team were out practicing, and they could hear the coxswain barking commands to his rowers and the splash of eight oars driving through the deep blue river.

"Let's turn here," Colin shouted, waving for Amy to follow him onto a winding dirt path.

Amy pedaled cautiously, remembering how she'd skidded on gravel not long before. She didn't need two falls in one week.

Colin led her to a bench overlooking the river. Thick bushes with glossy green leaves hid it from view.

"It's beautiful here," Amy said dreamily as she sat down beside Colin.

"I used to come here a lot when I was a kid. See down there?" Colin pointed to a rock in the distance. "That's where I fished in the summer."

114

"Did you ever catch anything?"

"Just trouble — from my mom." Colin laughed. "She didn't exactly like me hanging around the deep water when I was so little."

"Do you swim a lot?" Amy asked.

"Yeah," Colin said. "That's one of the main reasons I like summer."

"I love swimming, too," she said. "My family used to rent a cabin by a lake in Vermont every summer. My dad taught me to swim there."

"Are you going this summer?" Colin asked.

Amy shook her head. "I don't think so. My parents just split up." She tried to deliver this lightly but didn't quite succeed. She knew her voice gave some of her feelings away. "I don't know what's going on about anything right now," she admitted.

Colin looked down at Amy, and his eyes softened. "I'm sorry to hear about your parents," he said. "That must be pretty hard on you."

"It is. I'm getting used to it, though. Divorce happens to lots of families these days."

"That doesn't make it any easier."

"I know, but there's comfort in numbers." Amy smiled at him. She appreciated his concern.

"Right." Colin smiled back.

Before Amy realized what was happening, Colin put his arm around her shoulder. With his other hand, he reached over and gently tilted her chin toward him. Slowly, softly he kissed her, then kissed her again.

Amy couldn't keep from melting toward him. Her whole body relaxed against his as if they'd been molded together. She could feel Colin's heart beat through his T-shirt. Lost in the sensation of his closeness, she rested her hand on his arm and pressed herself even more tightly against him.

But when Colin's lips sought hers even more hungrily, Amy suddenly realized what she was doing. No matter how much she wanted to, she couldn't erase Susan's image from her mind. What was she doing betraying Susan this way? Amy stiffened slightly despite the warmth of Colin's arms.

With every bit of determination she could muster, she moved her hand to Colin's chest and pushed herself away. She wanted to sink against him again, hold him close as long as she could, but she just couldn't do it. Not when she felt so guilty about her sister.

"Colin, I have to go," Amy said abruptly. As soon as she spoke, she felt embarrassed and silly. This wasn't how it was supposed to be when a girl found herself kissing the boy she'd been dreaming about. But Amy couldn't possibly explain to Colin what was really going on.

"I love being with you," she backtracked, feeling completely torn. "I mean, this has been fun. . . . But I really can't stay."

"But Amy — "

"No, really," Amy insisted. "I'm sorry. I wish I didn't have to go."

Colin held onto Amy's hand as she stood up quickly. "Have I done anything wrong?" he asked, his eyebrows slanted in puzzlement.

Forcing herself to leave was one of the hardest things she'd ever done in her life. But without looking back, Amy walked quickly to her bike, and her escape from this confusion.

"I'll see you tomorrow night at Marc's party," Colin called after her.

His voice echoed through Amy's mind the whole way home.

Chapter *13*

Colin leaned back against the bench, crossed his arms over his chest, and watched Amy ride off on her bicycle. I must have offended her somehow, he thought. No, that can't be it. She seemed like she wanted to kiss me as much as I wanted to kiss her.

But then why did she leave so suddenly? Colin shook his head. The question bothered him, but he couldn't come up with any answer. Once Amy was out of sight, he looked down at the river and tried to figure out what was going on. Amy might like someone else and not want to get involved with him, he decided. Maybe she just wasn't interested in him romantically. That was always possible.

And yet she'd seemed really glad to go for a bike ride, and she certainly hadn't tried to stop him from kissing her. Colin couldn't figure her out.

At least he knew he'd have a chance to see her at Marc's party tomorrow. Maybe he could talk to her then and find out what she was thinking.

Amy was a fantastic girl; he *was* sure about that. And he really wanted to get to know her better. The last thing in the world he intended was to upset her and maybe threaten their new friendship. He'd have to clear things up between them right away.

Colin looked at his watch. Twenty-seven-and-a-half hours until the party. He couldn't remember ever caring so much about a social event in his life. He was sure glad he'd made it onto the invitation list of this one!

His mind shifted to a more practical matter. If he left now he'd have time to get some computer paper on his way home. Rose Hill Office Supplies was just two blocks from his house. He got up from the bench quickly and started off on his bicycle.

As he approached the shopping area of downtown Rose Hill, the traffic got heavier. Colin stuck close to the side of the road so cars could easily pass. He made a hand signal to turn onto Jefferson Avenue, headed up the block toward the office supply store, and looked for a place to park his bike.

Just as he locked it to a parking meter, he glanced across the street and saw Susan getting off at the bus stop, her red-and-white polka-dot skirt blowing against her knees in the wind. She really looks a lot like Amy, Colin thought as he watched her. Anyone could easily tell they were sisters. It's funny, though, Colin thought, that people can look alike on the surface and be so different underneath. Susan was a great girl, but she wasn't Amy. She didn't have the same soft eyes and gentle smile. She didn't make Colin feel inside the way Amy did — like it was Christmas morning and he was just about to open the most wonderful present in the world.

Colin wanted to find out how Susan did on her math test today. He cut across the street toward her.

"Hey, Susan," he called as soon as he got closer.

Susan looked over at him. Her face brightened with a huge smile.

"Colin! I have to talk to you." She ran out into the cross walk to meet him.

"Guess what!?" she asked, breathless, her ponytail bouncing as she ran.

"What?"

"I had my algebra test today," she said and turned to walk back to the curb with him.

"I know. How'd you do?"

"Fantastic! I'm sure I did."

"That's great, Susan." Colin smiled at her. "I bet you'll turn that F around."

"I *know* I will," Susan declared, her cheeks glowing. "The problems were really easy. A couple of them were almost exactly like what you and I did in the book!"

Colin reached over and gave Susan's ponytail another one of those affectionate, little-sister tugs. "We'll have to celebrate when you get your test back Monday," he said.

Susan grabbed his arm and squeezed it. "I

couldn't have done it without your help," she said and leaned so close to him he felt her body pressing against him.

When Colin looked down at her, he found her face turned up eagerly toward his and she looked as if she wanted to kiss him. Colin couldn't remember Susan's acting like this before. All of a sudden her friendliness made him a little ill at ease.

Whoa, he thought. Wait just a minute here. Suddenly everything became clear. Susan had a crush on him! And she wasn't even being subtle about it.

Though Colin was flattered, he didn't need to think twice about it. He knew Susan wasn't for him. Amy was. Looking down at Susan again, it occurred to him that Amy must know how Susan felt. Maybe that explained why Amy had left so quickly at the river. She'd wanted to kiss him, be with him, but she'd stopped because she knew Susan liked him

Colin stepped away quickly from Susan. She was a pretty girl. He liked her freckles and her ponytail. But she wasn't Amy.

Susan dropped her hand from Colin's arm but she still smiled up at him.

"Miss Taylor's going to be thrilled when she grades my test and sees how much better I'm doing," she said happily.

"I'm sure she will," Colin agreed, not so enthusiastically as before.

"I'll tell her what a great tutor you are!"

"Thanks."

"I can't wait to show you the test."

"Sure. Monday then." Colin took another step back.

Susan looked at him a little oddly. She must have noticed that he was suddenly more aloof.

"I've got to get some computer paper before the store closes," Colin said, turning away with a wave. "See you."

"Sure," Susan said. Her eyes didn't sparkle quite as much as they had a few moments before. "I'll see you on Monday, Colin." He felt her blue eyes on his back as he walked away, and he could almost see their hurt expression.

Amy carefully poured steaming water from a copper kettle into a bowl of strawberry Jell-O. Her mother had said she'd be home a little late, so Amy was getting dinner ready.

She was glad for the excuse to putter in the kitchen. She felt secure there, and right now she needed that feeling. Her whole world had just turned upside down.

Everything in her longed to be with Colin, to be able to go out with him if she wanted to without worrying about Susan. Every time she thought about his lips on hers, she shivered. The steam from the tea kettle was cold compared to the way Colin made her feel inside.

She stirred the Jell-O and watched it dissolve in the bottom of the bowl. If only her problems could all melt away so easily, she thought. She hadn't intended for her life to get so out of hand, and yet it was becoming more complicated practically by the minute.

Amy knew she should tell Susan she'd gone

biking with Colin, but there was no way she could mention Colin's kisses. Though the dishonesty really bothered her, she knew she'd only hurt her sister if she told her the truth.

She rehearsed a speech to Susan as she stirred. She and Colin had run into each other after school and decided to go riding. Now that he'd started tutoring Susan, he and Amy were also getting to be better friends. That was true, sort of. He and Amy had talked about how well Susan was doing in algebra and how happy they were for her. That was true, too.

Then Amy would let the subject drop. Susan shouldn't be too upset about them taking a bike ride together. And that, Amy hoped, would be the end of it.

But then she had to admit that it wouldn't. She still had to deal with Colin and with her own feelings for him. She had no idea how she was going to do that.

Amy shook her head in confusion and stirred even harder. Nothing was ever easy, she thought. Caring about someone — a boy *or* a sister — sure made life complicated.

When Amy heard Susan bound through the front door and slam it behind her, she braced herself. Wherever Susan went, she was like a whirlwind. Amy's father used to say she had enough energy to light up all of D.C.

With Sam waddling along behind her, Susan tossed her backpack on the dining room table with a thump and dashed into the kitchen.

"I just saw Colin," she said, but without the enthusiasm Amy would have expected.

Amy's body tensed at the words. "Where?" she asked, trying to sound indifferent.

"A few blocks from here. When I got off the bus." Susan sat down on a stool. "He seemed different today. I don't know, less friendly." She hooked her feet around the stool's wooden rungs. "You don't think he likes somebody else, do you, Amy?" she asked, tipping her head to one side and looking seriously at her sister.

Amy froze inside, but she managed to keep stirring, even though the Jell-O was ready to go into the refrigerator. Staring into the bowl was a lot better than seeing Susan's eyes.

"I really don't know, Susan," Amy said.

"I couldn't stand it if he did have someone," Susan continued, shaking her ponytail in dismay.

Amy felt so guilty she was sure it had to show. Now was definitely not the time to bring up the bike ride. "Maybe you should just wait and see what happens," she counseled, adopting her usual tone but without her usual sincerity. "He might just have had a bad day."

"Yeah." Susan sighed. "I've got to make him like me, Amy. I mean, I know he likes me *some*. But I want it to be *more*." She leaned over and put an elbow on the counter. "I thought maybe if I asked him to Casey's swimming party like I told you, we could get to know each other without talking about algebra."

Amy kept stirring mechanically. "Maybe so," she said softly.

Susan didn't seem to notice Amy's discomfort. "He's so cute," she went on. "I'd absolutely hate any girl he went out with if she weren't me!"

Susan jumped off the stool and crossed to the refrigerator for a carton of milk.

"He left pretty quickly today. Before I could ask him to the party," Susan said as she poured milk into a glass. "Maybe I'll call him tomorrow."

"Uh-huh," Amy said.

Susan took a sip of milk. "Anything wrong, Amy?"

"Oh, no. I'm just tired." Amy smiled a false smile.

Susan patted her affectionately on the shoulder. "I think I'll watch TV."

"Go ahead," Amy said as Susan headed toward the door.

Amy quickly put cellophane wrap over the Jell-O bowl and shoved it in the refrigerator. If she didn't get out of the house in two minutes, she might just explode. All she wanted was to be alone. Her room was out — Susan might come in to talk and Amy didn't trust herself to keep this secret under so much pressure.

Since she didn't feel like going for a bike ride, Amy took her gardening gloves from the kitchen drawer and slipped outside to the backyard. She'd already picked out a place for her garden, but she needed to hoe before she could plant anything.

She rustled up some tools from the garage and immediately started to work. Maybe I can bury all my feelings in the ground, she thought. I wish all my problems could be like dirt — I could turn them over and break them down and shovel them away.

But life wasn't like that. No matter what Amy

did now, she was sure Susan would never forgive her. Susan wouldn't be fooled if Amy told her that she and Colin were just friends, but lying wasn't right, either.

It had hurt to see Susan feeling rejected by Colin today. Now Amy was about to make everything even worse.

Amy knelt down and started pulling weeds. As she shook away the dirt that hung in clumps from the roots, she kept thinking and slowly her worries shifted from concern for Susan to concern for herself. Didn't she have as much right to be happy as Susan? Wasn't she the one Colin had wanted to be with today? Did she have to sacrifice her own feelings for her sister's just because she'd always felt so responsible for Susan?

That familiar all-mixed-up feeling came back to Amy again. She smoothed her hand over the earth. Colin's tomato plants would go in a row right where she was working. She could hardly wait to get them.

Amy thought again about kissing him, and that same shiver went through her. She'd never felt anything so good as being in his arms. How could she possibly give that up? But how could she ever hurt Susan so deeply?

Chapter
14

When Susan left Saturday morning for a friend's house, Amy breathed a deep sigh of relief. At least she wouldn't have to spend the day guiltily avoiding her own sister. Amy knew she couldn't pretend to be indifferent through any more conversations about Colin, but she had no idea how else to act.

When Susan came home for dinner, Amy gathered up all her discipline like a suit of armor and marched downstairs to the kitchen, determined not to reveal her emotions. She ate her fried chicken and potato salad in silence, hoping Susan and her mother would keep up their chatter about the unpacking they planned to do that night.

Finally, after what Amy figured was the most difficult dinner she could remember since her parents announced their divorce, she hurried to her room to wrap Marc's birthday present. It was just a bag of gourmet bubble gum since Dee had in-sisted no gift should cost more than two dollars.

Susan's voice followed her up the steps to her room. "If you see Colin at the party, say hi for me!"

Amy tripped. "Sure, Susan," she called back.

She sighed. It looked like no matter where she turned or what she did, she was going to be re-minded of her terrible predicament. She just couldn't escape it. She'd be leaving Susan inno-cently at home and going where she knew she'd be seeing Colin. She knew she should feel bad about that, and she knew she should be worried, too. Colin might want to talk about what had happened yesterday by the river and she wasn't sure what she'd say. But despite everything, Amy was just plain excited to see him. She couldn't help it.

The evening would be fun no matter what had happened between her and Colin, she reminded herself. Dee had been thrilled when Amy had called to say Marc was coming after all. And the whole crowd would be there to meet him. Amy could hardly wait to see the expression on Marc's face when he walked in.

In her bedroom she put his bubble gum into a shiny, flowered bag and tied it up with a white yarn bow. Then she went to the bathroom and ran water for a hot bath. With all the tension she'd been under, sinking down into the tub was heaven. She lay in the water for a few luxurious minutes.

Later she worked carefully on her makeup. No matter what was about to happen at Dee's party,

Amy had to look her best. She put tiny smudges of soft blue shadow on her eyelids, swiped away at her lashes with brown mascara, and then bent toward the mirror to look closely at the results.

Not bad, she thought, and smiled at her reflection. Her soft blonde hair shone under the bathroom light and her skin looked radiant. Nobody would ever be able to tell she was in an upheaval over Susan and Colin. A dab of blusher and some lipstick and gloss were all she needed to look perfectly together, on the outside at least.

Amy went back to her room and started to dress. Because she needed an extra bit of confidence tonight, she decided to wear her favorite outfit: a pale blue cotton dress gathered at the waist, with a loose, blousy top that fell slightly off her shoulders.

Perfect, she thought a few minutes later when she examined herself from head to foot in the mirror on the back of her closet door. She had to admit she looked really good. She smiled with excitement.

In spite of her apprehension about Colin, the excitement stayed with her as she drove to Dee's house. She parked a few blocks away so Marc wouldn't see her mother's car and hurried to Dee's front door to ring the doorbell.

"Marc should be here in a few minutes," Dee said, hugging Amy. "Hurry back to the kitchen! Everybody's hiding there."

As Amy rushed through Dee's living room, she noticed the Happy Birthday sign above the fireplace and the refreshments all spread out on the dining room table. Dee had obviously taken great care with every detail. Marc would be so touched, Amy was sure.

Before she even got to the kitchen, she heard the crowd's giggles and hoots.

"You're going to have to be quieter than this," Amy warned as she opened the door. "Marc'll hear you a mile away!"

Woody jumped toward her with a huge rubber dog's nose attached to his face. "Surprise!" he shouted and tried to sniff at her neck.

Amy laughed. "Come on, Woody, it's not Halloween!"

"You can't get ready for it too early," Woody said. Kim gave him a playful slap. "I found this at the Nature Company today."

"You mean that's not your real nose?" Jeremy asked, keeping a straight face. "I never would have known."

"Any more wise cracks, and I'll wolf up all the food." Woody shook a finger at Jeremy.

Amy glanced across the kitchen and saw Colin standing near the refrigerator toward the back of the crowd. He was watching her intently. He looked serious, as if he had more on his mind than just the party. When his eyes met hers, though, he smiled in his usual warm way, and Amy waved to him. She tried to look calm, even if she was feeling exactly the opposite.

"The rules are that we've got to shut up till Marc gets to the living room," Ben instructed Amy. "Then we're supposed to stampede through the door and yell 'Surprise!' "

"With Woody's nose, Marc'll be surprised for sure," Elise said reaching for Ben's hand.

"Did any of you guys spill the beans to Marc?" Bart asked. "He's still in the dark, isn't he?"

"As far as I know," Kim said. "I talked to him this afternoon. He didn't seem to suspect a thing."

Suddenly Dee rushed through the kitchen door. "Shhh!" she ordered, her finger to her lips and her eyes wide. "Everybody be quiet! Marc's parking his car in front of the house."

The crowd hushed instantly and she hurried back to the living room.

The doorbell rang several times, and the kitchen filled with muffled giggles and more "shhh's." Excitement crackled through the room while everyone waited.

Dee's voice drifted through the closed kitchen door. She innocently greeted Marc as if tonight were just any average Saturday. Only Amy knew how hard it must have been for Dee to act as if nothing had been wrong between her and Marc the past few days.

As Marc's voice got louder, everyone could tell he was walking into the living room.

"Come on, troops," Woody hissed.

With shouts and more giggles, the whole crowd pushed and shoved their way through the narrow kitchen door.

"Surprise!" rang through the living room.

Marc's head turned so fast his neck nearly snapped. His eyes widened and his jaw dropped. Without saying a word, he stood completely stunned and watched all his best friends barreling toward him.

131

"Hey, Marc, what'dya think, it's your birthday or something?" Woody yelled.

Still silent, Marc turned and looked down at Dee in disbelief.

"Happy birthday," she said softly, reaching up on tiptoes to kiss him lightly on the cheek.

By then the whole crowd surrounded Marc. Slowly his shock changed to laughter. Dee and Amy gave each other a knowing look. Marc's reaction was the evidence they needed that the party was going to be a huge success. Even if Marc *had* been strange all week, even if they'd had a terrible time getting him to come tonight, he was certainly happy now.

"Okay, gang," Monica Ford's voice came loud and clear over the speakers that were set up in the corners of Dee's living room. "We can't stand here all night looking at each other. It's time for some serious dancing!"

With that, Bruce Springsteen blasted from the stereo, and the room filled with cheers again.

When the lights went down and everyone started dancing, Marc put his arm around Dee's shoulders and led her into the kitchen where they could be alone.

The minute the door was closed behind them, he scooped her up into his arms and kissed her gently on the lips.

"Thanks, Dee," he said, smiling down at her, his eyes glowing.

"I *wanted* to tell you what was going on." Dee rubbed her nose against his cheek and giggled. "But obviously I couldn't."

132

"I had no idea," Marc said, shaking his head in amazement.

"I know. I wish I'd had my camera ready. You should have seen the look on your face when everybody came into the room."

"Did my mouth fall open enough for flies to get in?"

"Just a few hundred," Dee teased. It felt so good to have Marc back to his old self again. "I was so afraid you'd find out," she added.

"I can't believe I didn't."

"We thought you might suspect something when everybody kept casually asking what you were doing tonight."

Marc suddenly looked a little guilty. "I'm really sorry I said I couldn't come."

"That's okay. You just scared me to death, that's all." Dee smiled wryly.

"I was just mad." Marc shook his head and squeezed her shoulders more tightly. "You *have* been acting weird lately."

"*I've* been weird?" Dee gasped.

"Yeah." Marc laughed at her surprise. "But now I see why."

"What do you mean?"

"You've been distracted, with the party and everything." His voice became serious. "I guess I owe you an apology."

"You don't have to apologize," Dee said, giving him a gentle kiss on the cheek. "I have been distracted, and I wasn't really aware of the way you've been feeling lately — I mean with your grandmother being sick and all. We just weren't communicating very well."

"You can say that again," Marc agreed emphatically.

Dee didn't want to think about all the problems she and Marc had been having all week. Tonight wasn't the time to talk about them. They'd had a terrible misunderstanding, that was all. She wanted to forget it ever happened.

Marc rumpled Dee's hair affectionately as he often did when he was about to say something important without coming across too seriously. "I still think you work too hard on *The Red and the Gold*," he whispered, smiling. "I've been wanting to talk to you about it for a long time."

Dee raised her chin in mock defiance. "You can't criticize my hobbies when you're such a soccer fanatic! You play *all the time*. Even when it's not soccer season!" she declared.

"Okay, peace!" Marc laughed.

"We have to try and spend more time together," Dee said.

"Do you promise?" Marc asked, looking deep into her eyes, his own eyes more serious than she'd ever seen them.

"Cross my heart."

"Then everything's okay," Mark bent down and kissed her softly on the mouth again. The sparks between them sent a blaze clear down to Dee's bones. Their kisses grew more urgent, as if they were telling each other how much they cared and how glad they were they'd made up again.

When a loud burst of laughter came from the living room, Marc pulled back with a look of regret in his eyes. "I wish we could stay here for the rest of the night," he said, his voice low and warm.

"We'd better get back to the party." Dee smiled up at him, her arms still around his neck. "We'll have some private time alone soon to talk, I'll make sure of it."

They went back to join their friends in the living room.

"Okay, folks, don't forget there's plenty of food on the table," Monica announced as she changed records.

"You'd better believe it!" Woody shouted and charged toward the table loaded with Kim's little pizzas.

Amy didn't really hear much of the banter around the refreshment table. She and Colin were dancing in the corner of the room.

Holding each other close during the slow, dreamy music felt so natural to Amy. Everything in her told her that she was exactly where she wanted to be. She leaned against Colin's strong body and reveled in the way his arms held her so securely.

But when he'd asked her to dance, she'd promised herself she wouldn't let him know how she was feeling, and this holding back put her completely on edge.

So much still hadn't been said — about Susan and particularly about Amy's running away yesterday afternoon. Amy kept waiting for Colin to bring up the subject. Expecting any minute to have to explain herself made her tense in spite of her pleasure at being so close to him again.

When the music ended, Colin rested his chin on top of her head. The gesture was so affectionate and familiar it made Amy feel as if they'd been going out together for months. She wanted to nestle against his chest but she stopped herself. No matter what she did, she couldn't shake Susan from her consciousness. Her sister may as well have been standing between her and Colin, pushing them apart. The warm sensation of Colin's nearness got tangled up with Amy's feelings of confusion and guilt.

As if reading her mind, Colin leaned down and whispered in her ear. "I want to talk to you, Amy. Let's go sit out on the back porch for a while, okay?"

Amy hesitated. She wanted to talk to him more than anything, but she was a little scared. She wasn't sure what he wanted to say or what *she* wanted to say in response.

"Okay," she said finally.

Colin took her hand and slowly made his way through the crowd toward the kitchen. "There's a door to the porch somewhere back here," he said.

Amy knew all about that door. The last time she'd used it was when she'd snuck over to Dee's a few days before, hoping she wouldn't run into Colin and be exposed in her lie about going to the dentist.

Outside, the air was warm and heavy with the scent of springtime. Tall maple trees cast long shadows in the yard. The moon shone through the branches, leaving a trail of soft light on the porch steps.

Amy sat down on the top stair, and Colin fit himself so close to her their thighs touched. Amy felt a surge of warmth go through her whole body. The electricity between them grew even stronger when Colin reached over and took her hand.

They sat quietly for a moment, looking out into Dee's backyard. Then Colin turned to Amy. "Are you going out with anyone?" he asked abruptly.

"No," Amy answered, a little shocked by his question. "Why do you ask?"

"When you left in such a rush yesterday, I thought it might be because you were dating somebody," Colin explained, shrugging shyly.

"No." Amy shook her head vehemently. She sighed. "It's just that everything's so *complicated*."

"Do you want to talk about it, or am I prying?

Amy smiled weakly. "You're not prying. I just don't know how to talk about it, that's all." She paused a moment and looked at the maple trees for moral support. "I don't know what to do about it, either."

"You mean about us?"

Hearing Colin refer to them as "us" was thrilling to Amy, and yet it put more pressure on her.

"I guess so," she said, feeling more torn than ever.

Without letting go of Amy's hand, Colin leaned forward and rested his elbow on his knee. His eyes never left Amy's. "I saw Susan yesterday at the bus stop," he began. "From the way she was acting, I kind of got the feeling she liked me. Was I right?"

Amy's shoulders tensed slightly. "I can't really talk about it. She's my sister. And — "

"But I really need to know," Colin insisted.

Amy hesitated again. She couldn't avoid the issue now that Colin had brought it up, but she still had Susan to consider. Was Amy hurting her sister more by admitting Susan had a crush on Colin than she would be by dancing with him and feeling more and more that she was really falling in love? Any way she looked at it, she was double-dealing.

Amy inhaled deeply and looked up at the moon again. "Okay," she said, then paused. "Susan likes you a lot. Actually, she's crazy about you."

Colin didn't look the least bit surprised. "And you're trying to keep your distance from me because you don't want to be disloyal?"

"Yes," Amy admitted. "But obviously it's not doing any good." She looked down at their fingers entwining. "There's not a whole lot of distance between us now anyway."

Colin grinned at her. "You bet there's not." He let go of her hand and put his arm around her shoulders. "I'm sure glad there isn't."

Just as he'd done yesterday afternoon, Colin tilted Amy's chin up toward him. Nothing in her could possibly resist him now. He kissed her softly on her forehead, then her nose, and finally settled on her mouth. Her lips met his just as eagerly as they had before. The same warmth and excitement that had flowed between them was as strong now as it had been yesterday by the river.

"Amy," Colin whispered, his lips brushing against her temple. "Don't you understand?"

138

"Hum?" Amy asked, lost in the sensation of his closeness.

"It's you I care about. Susan's great, and I like her a lot. But you're the one I want."

Before Amy could say anything, Colin put his other arm around her and held her close again. She reveled in the soft touch of his hands and the smoothness of his cheek against hers. The cool spring air, to Amy, began to feel like summer sunshine. Colin's hug warmed her clear through.

"I've been wanting to hold you like this since I was at your house last week," Colin whispered. "You were sitting in your living room with the leg injury from falling off your bike. You were so *cute!*"

"Mmmm," Amy mumbled, pressing her cheek against his chest. "That's when I started liking you, too."

When she looked up, Colin kissed her again, then slowly pulled back from her. "Are you really that worried about Susan?"

"I just can't help it," she said. "She told me yesterday she'd hate anyone who went out with you."

"But she wouldn't hate her own sister."

"Well, she's been pretty upset since our parents got divorced. Meeting you has been the first thing that's made her happy again." Amy shook her head sadly.

Colin brushed a hand over her hair reassuringly. "Even if she's mad, she'll get over it," he said. "She's not going to sit around and pout until you go off to college."

Amy smiled at him. "I hope not."

"Let's talk to her Monday when I come to tutor," he suggested. "We can tell her how much we like each other. We'll get it out in the open and then the worst will be over with."

"Okay," Amy agreed reluctantly. She really had no choice. She could never deny her feelings for Colin now, and Susan was bound to find out.

"In the meantime, we've got a party to enjoy," Colin said, grinning at her.

"Right." Amy grinned back.

"But I'd sure rather sit here with you."

After Colin kissed her again, they held each other quietly in the moonlight, enjoying being so close and so comfortable with each other. Colin pushed a stray curl back behind Amy's ear. "Don't worry, Amy," he said softly, looking down into her eyes. "We'll manage Susan somehow."

But Amy still wasn't sure.

Chapter
15

The next morning Amy woke up early. She went downstairs to fix breakfast and found her mother standing at the stove, stirring up a batch of oatmeal.

" 'Morning, Mom," Amy said.

Mrs. Atkinson looked up from the bubbling cereal. "Hi, honey. You still look pretty sleepy."

"I am." Amy yawned. She poured herself a glass of orange juice and sat down at the kitchen table.

"Did you have fun last night?" her mother asked.

"Uh-*huh*," Amy replied enthusiastically. She'd have really liked to tell her mother about it.

"Was Marc surprised?"

"You should have seen him! He couldn't believe it."

"That's good." Mrs. Atkinson pulled the tie of her white terry cloth robe tighter around her waist, picked up the pot of oatmeal, and spooned out two healthy servings into flowered china bowls.

"I guess Susan's still asleep," she said as she carried the oatmeal to the table.

"She's up," Amy replied. "I heard her messing around in her room over an hour ago. I could've killed her for waking me up so early!"

"I wonder why she hasn't come down yet? The oatmeal will get cold."

Amy took her bowl and sprinkled on a few raisins and a spoonful of sugar. She could never remember feeling so warm inside or so happy as she had last night with Colin. But pretty soon they had to face Susan, and Amy had no idea how that confrontation was going to work out. And she still had to make it through the rest of the weekend in the same house with her sister, who had no idea of what was going on. Being dishonest for the next twenty-four hours wasn't going to be any easier than it had been all week long.

"Did you dance a lot last night?" Amy's mother asked, interrupting her thoughts.

"Sure," Amy said and grinned at her mother. "It was wonderful."

"And you didn't drive Mr. and Mrs. Patterson crazy with too much noise?" Mrs. Atkinson teased.

Amy rolled her eyes. "No, Mom. They didn't complain once."

Amy spooned out a big bite of oatmeal and waited for it to cool enough to swallow. As she watched the steam curling up in a thin white wisp, Susan burst into the kitchen in her pink-and-white tennis outfit, with Sam waddling along behind on short, pudgy legs.

" 'Morning!" Susan said, her ponytail bouncing.

"You look awfully chipper," her mother said. "There's oatmeal for you on the stove."

"Great!" Susan bounded over to the pan and energetically spooned out the last of the cereal.

"How was the party?" She asked Amy as she pulled a chair out beside her.

"Fine," Amy said, trying to tone down her enthusiasm.

"Was Colin there?"

"Sure. He's good friends with Marc."

"You said hello, for me, didn't you?"

Amy gulped. She couldn't avoid lying again. "Uh-huh," she said noncommittally.

"What'd he say?"

"Oh." Amy paused. She stared at the vase of flowers in the center of the table for inspiration. "I think we talked about how well you were doing in algebra."

"Good!" Susan said. She started heartily in on her oatmeal.

"The algebra's going well, honey?" Mrs. Atkinson inquired.

"Fantastic! I bet I got an A on my test Friday. Colin seemed really happy about it, too."

"Just get those grades up," her mother warned gently.

Susan stopped eating for a moment and turned in her chair toward her sister. "By the way, was Colin there with anybody last night?" she asked.

Amy winced. Susan's face looked so vulnerable and eager. All Amy could think of was how much she wanted to get out of the kitchen before her sister could ask any more questions and force her into more lies.

"He didn't come with anyone," Amy said. That was true enough.

"Did he seem like he was interested in anybody?"

The spoonful of oatmeal Amy tried to swallow got stuck in her throat. She reached for her orange juice.

"Are you okay?" her mother asked.

"Uh-huh," Amy said, hoping Susan would forget her question.

"Could you tell if Colin likes anyone especially?" Susan persisted when Amy had stopped coughing.

"Not really," Amy said. "I mean, how should I know?"

"You were there. You saw him," Susan pointed out reasonably.

"I don't know, Susan. I couldn't tell."

Amy got up from the table and shoved the rest of her oatmeal down the garbage disposal. Not finishing breakfast was preferable to dodging Susan's questions, that was for sure.

"I'm going to go hit some balls against the backboard," Susan said to her mother as she scraped her bowl clean.

"Where?" Mrs. Atkinson asked.

"On Maple Avenue." Susan giggled. "The courts are a block from Colin's."

Amy put her bowl into the dishwasher and darted out of the kitchen. She could still hear Susan talking to her mother as she climbed the stairs to her room.

"Maybe I'll run into Colin playing tennis there, too," Susan was saying.

Half an hour later, after riding past Colin's house on her bicycle, Susan arrived at the neighborhood courts. She'd hoped maybe Colin would be outside, washing the family car or mowing the lawn. But from the street, his house looked as if no one were home and she had to admit there probably wasn't much chance that he'd be playing tennis.

It was still too early on a Sunday morning for many people to be on the courts. In fact, Susan had the backboard to herself. She unzipped her carrying case and took out her racket. Soon she was whacking a ball with a thud against the board and running back and forth to keep the rally going.

The sun warmed her up fast. It was a beautiful day. The only thing that would make it better, Susan thought, was if Colin suddenly arrived at the courts and started playing tennis with her.

Just as she was thinking about that prospect, a lanky blond boy walked up near her and dropped his bag of gear on the concrete. From Susan's short height, he looked incredibly tall, she figured at least six feet two. She could tell from his build that he was an athlete. The strong muscles in his upper arms pressed against his red T-shirt.

Susan kept up her rally at the backboard, but between swipes at the ball, she watched the boy out of the corner of her eye. If she couldn't be around Colin today, he was surely a good substitute. Several times she almost missed her ball because she kept looking at him, completely drawn to his blond good looks.

He walked casually over beside her at the backboard.

"Mind if I hit a few, too?" he called to her.

"Be my guest," Susan answered, grinning at him.

Soon both of them were slamming their balls against the board with so much energy it shuddered. But then Susan's ball hit at an angle and bounced over toward the boy. She took a flying leap to save the shot, but she was too late. The ball flew across the court and landed against the fence with a clunk.

Susan started to run behind him to retrieve her ball, but just then *his* ball bounced over toward her. She lifted her racket and batted it back against the board to him.

"Hey, good shot!" he said. He took aim and hit it back against the board to her again.

Susan ran forward to get his shot. After another few shots, they were hitting the ball back and forth to each other as if they'd spent every Sunday morning for years warming up for tennis this way.

"Hey, you're good!" the boy shouted as he ran to hit the ball.

"So are you," Susan answered.

"Want to play a game? Some courts are open."

"Sure," Susan said.

He caught the ball easily with one hand. "How about over there?" he asked and nodded to an empty court near them.

"Great!" Susan said. If Colin drove by now, maybe he'd get jealous, she thought. But then this boy was so cute, all of a sudden she wasn't sure she cared so much how Colin felt.

For the next half hour, Susan played tennis for all she was worth. She'd always won tournaments at summer camp, and she knew she was a good player, but her partner was definitely her match.

"Eat your heart out," he yelled with a crooked grin when she accidentally batted the ball so far it landed way out.

"I'll get you. Just wait!" she laughed back.

And she did. After several more games they were still tied. The sun got hotter overhead, and Susan was breathing heavily from the exercise. But she didn't let him get the advantage even though she was starting to feel exhausted.

When it was his turn to serve, he stopped for a minute. "Had enough? Or are you a glutton for punishment?" he asked her with a confident smile.

"How about *you*? You can't fool me. You're stepping on your tongue!"

They laughed easily together as if they'd known each other for years. Susan had never felt so comfortable with a guy right off the bat, but that wasn't all she was feeling. Looking at his strong, lanky body, she had to resist an urge to jump over the net and hug him. If she hadn't had to concentrate on returning his shots, she'd have easily started fantasizing about warm summer nights, watching the moon rise over the river with his arms around her.

"Let's go get a Coke or something. You want to?" he asked. "We'll call it a tie."

"Sure!" Susan said.

Together they walked over to the sidelines and packed up their gear.

He reached out his hand to shake Susan's. "Good game," he said. "I wish I could apologize for beating you."

"But you can't," she said, teasing.

"I'm not too proud to say I've met my match." He zipped up the cover of his tennis racket. "Do you live nearby? I just live around the corner — over there," he said and waved over to the left.

"Oh, you live nearby? You must know Colin Edwards," Susan answered.

"*Know* him?" the boy laughed. "He's my brother!"

"You're Rich *Edwards*?" Susan gasped. "Colin's brother?" She burst out laughing. "I'm Susan *Atkinson* — we were supposed to go out last night!"

"I can't believe this," Rich said, still laughing.

Susan stared at him in amazement. If this were Rich Edwards, she was sorry now she'd turned down the date. He was adorable. Every bit as cute as Colin and even more fun.

She and Rich hopped on their bikes and rode together to the mall. A few minutes later they were sitting at a cozy round table in the ice-cream parlor.

Susan barely saw the pink-and-white striped walls or the feathery green ferns that hung from the ceiling near the windows. She barely tasted her chocolate milk shake. She couldn't take her eyes off Rich.

"So you're on the soccer team with Marc," she said as she rolled the straw between her fingers.

"Since last fall," he said nodding. "Coach picked me out of one of his PE classes to join the team."

"You could be on the tennis team if you wanted to," Susan said.

"So could you." Rich put his elbows on the table and leaned toward her. "Why aren't you, anyway?"

"My grades," Susan said, wishing she didn't have to talk about them. "Dad said I shouldn't spend too much time on other things if I couldn't keep a good B average."

"I know what you mean," Rich said, then laughed. "Those C's do have a way of sneaking onto report cards."

"You get them, too?" Amy asked, smiling.

"Yeah. It's kind of grim with Colin around. He's always on the honor roll."

"So's my sister."

"Then you know what it's like." Rich gave her a knowing look.

Susan certainly did know. It wasn't always easy having a brain for a sister. "Do you play any other sports?" Susan asked.

"Just soccer and tennis. And I swim all summer."

"So do I," Susan said.

"The Park and Rec Department just hired me as a life guard starting in June."

"Fantastic!" Susan couldn't help thinking how much fun it would be going to the pool with Rich around. She could see him every single day this summer if she wanted to. They could splash around in the water together, or she could bring him picnic lunches. It all sounded too good to be true.

Rich glanced down at his runner's watch, which was identical to Susan's, only larger. "I'm supposed to meet my parents by noon," he said. "We're going to a science exhibit at the Smithsonian."

"Sounds like something my sister would like."

"Colin, too. He and Dad are the science freaks in the family. Mom and I just go along for the ride."

Susan laughed. "I know what you mean."

For the first time since they'd met, Rich's face got a little serious. He chewed a piece of ice from his Coke. "Marc said you couldn't go out last night," he said slowly. "But would you like to do something next Saturday?"

"Sure!" Susan said eagerly. She wished now she hadn't said she'd had plans last night, but she couldn't admit to Rich that she'd turned him down because of his brother.

"Maybe we can go to a movie or something," Rich suggested, and when Susan smiled at him, he smiled back with equal warmth.

A few minutes later Susan rode with him to

his house, then waved good-bye, and headed for her own. Colin hadn't been outside when she passed this time, either. But Susan didn't mind a bit. She was sure going out with Rich next weekend would be the best thing that had happened to her in a long time.

As Susan pedaled home, she got even more excited about Rich. Bubbling over with enthusiasm, she rushed in the front door and looked for Amy to tell her the good news.

She hurried upstairs to Amy's room but didn't find her sister. Then she raced back down to the kitchen. Maybe Amy would be having lunch. Soon Susan realized her sister must have gone somewhere.

Disappointed, Susan decided to fix herself a sandwich. When she went to the refrigerator, she found a note on the door:

Susan,
 I've gone to pick up a few things at the store. Back by two. Amy decided to spend the day with your dad. Fix yourself a good lunch.

Love, Mom

So she'd just have to keep all her happiness inside for a while, Susan thought. She hugged herself and danced around the kitchen. Maybe everything would work out with Rich. He seemed to like her. And she certainly liked him. All she could think about was how great it would be to have a boyfriend like him this summer. They could go to movies and meet their friends by the river for picnics and watch softball games in the evenings.

It was funny how life worked out sometimes. Susan really had thought she'd fallen in love with Colin. But something even better had literally been waiting right around the corner — at the tennis courts!

By the time Susan finally fixed her sandwich and settled down to eat, she'd decided she was more excited than she'd ever been in her life.

Chapter
16

Dee had a hard time concentrating on Mr. Turner's lecture. History had never exactly been her favorite subject, and she was never very alert on Monday mornings anyway. Besides, she'd been so wrapped up in Marc's party and all her other activities for the past few days that she was dead tired, not to mention the fact that she'd barely skimmed today's assignment.

She glanced at the blossoming tree outside the classroom window for a moment without really seeing it. Her mind was still on Saturday night.

Marc had seemed so happy about the party. When he'd blown out the candles on his cake, she'd never seen him look so pleased. He'd loved all the silly presents everyone had brought, to say nothing of the calculator, and the picture she'd given him. And before he'd left that night, he'd kissed her over and over again. Dee had never felt so close to him before.

153

Everyone in the crowd had had a great time. All Kim's food had been devoured, Monica's music had been nothing less than fantastic, and Dee was especially pleased at how well Colin and Amy had gotten along.

Giving parties is fun, Dee thought. Even better is showing someone you love how much you care. All her trouble with Marc the week before had evaporated in her mind like so much fog on a sunny day. Now she and Marc were more in love than ever.

Suddenly feeling something was wrong, Dee snapped back to the reality of her history class. She looked up and found Mr. Turner standing right next to her desk.

"Here's your test," he said, laying it on her desk. "You didn't seem to hear me call your name."

As Mr. Turner moved on, Dee opened the folded paper and looked for her grade. On the bottom of the last page she found a C with so many minuses they went off the edge of the paper.

What's going on with you, Dee? Mr. Turner had scrawled in his crooked handwriting. *Aren't you studying anymore?*

Dee inhaled sharply. Seeing a grade like that shocked her. She'd never gotten anything lower than a B in her life, even in a subject she found as dull as history.

When Mr. Turner finished handing out the tests, he stopped at the front of the room. "Some of you didn't do too well on this exam," he said. "I certainly hope you'll study harder."

Dee couldn't help noticing he was looking straight at her.

Okay, she thought. You're right, Mr. Turner. She had to admit she'd been pretty caught up in other things lately. It was a mistake to let her grades go down the drain.

She looked down at her test again. That C- - - might as well have been shaking her by the shoulders and warning her she needed more balance in her life between work and play and love. Marc had been right. Dee *had* been too busy lately.

When the bell rang, Dee raced for the cafeteria to find Marc. He was sitting with the crowd at their usual table. But today instead of being in the middle of the group, instead of sitting as far away from her as possible, he was at the end, right next to the place he'd saved for her, He'd also set a cookie at her spot for her dessert.

"That's for you." Marc nodded at the cookie. "Mom baked a bunch last night. I wanted you to taste one."

Dee grinned down at him. He was acting so differently from last week. "Thanks," she said. "That's really thoughtful of you."

"Just want to keep you happy," Marc said and grinned back at her. He reached for her hand and squeezed it.

Dee looked at the others and realized she really wanted to be alone with Marc. "Want to eat outside?" she suggested. "It's such a beautiful day."

"Sure!" Marc picked up his bag lunch and Dee's cookie and followed her out to the sunshine.

"Let's go over by the soccer field." Dee pointed to a spot in the distance.

Holding hands, she and Marc walked along the sidewalk. The sky was bright blue with a few cottony clouds. Robins pecked at seeds in the grass. To Dee, the day was about as perfect as she'd ever seen. And it was all the better having Marc with her, especially now that they were getting along so well again.

They climbed up the steps of the bleachers by the soccer field and found a perfect place to sit in the sun at the top, overlooking the school grounds.

Dee looked down from where they sat. "Now you see what it's like watching you play from way up here," she said. Marc laughed.

Dee unpacked her tuna fish sandwich and took a bite while Marc dumped two sandwiches from his brown bag onto his lap. Before he started eating, he pulled the solar-powered calculator Dee had given him out of his shirt pocket.

"Let me show you how great this works," he said.

"We've sure got all the sun we need to operate it!" Dee said.

"It doesn't really need sun. Any light gets it going," Marc said. "Now look." He started punching a string of numbers. "The total is 113," he said proudly.

"What's eight times six?" Dee asked.

Marc whizzed through the calculation. "Do you want to figure out the square root of the sum of our teeth?" he joked.

"I've never been desperate to know that number," Dee teased back. "But I'm glad you like your present."

After a few more square roots and divisions, Marc put the calculator back in his pocket, and Dee, taking a sip of the juice in her thermos, looked out again across the soccer field.

"The practice game Saturday was great. You guys are going to have a great season next fall," she said. "I was so proud of you."

Marc put his arm around her shoulders and gave her a hug. "I was glad you were there."

"I developed the film yesterday. There's a super shot of you running down the field. I was thinking about having it blown up to life-size for my wall."

"Are you kidding?" Mark laughed. "You want me staring down at you all the time while you study?"

"Nothing better," Dee said and leaned against him.

"You know what, Marc?" she asked.

"Hmmm?"

"I got my history test back today."

"The one you had last week?"

"Uh-huh."

"How'd you do?"

"Brace yourself," she said, giggling.

"An A-plus?"

"Nope. Guess again."

"Was it bad?" Marc asked.

"A C-minus-minus-minus-minus-minus-minus. . . ." Dee kept listing off the minuses like a broken record.

"Hey, stop!" Marc put a hand over her lips.

"What'd Turner do? Write them all over the page?"

"Just about!"

He looked down at her with an affectionate smile, and then pretended to look stern. "You won't make a grade like that again, will you?" he asked, shaking his finger at her.

"No." Dee leaned even closer against him again. "I've been thinking, Marc," she began, then paused. "I mean, you were right. I *have* been spending too much time on photography. And your party. It was more obvious then ever when I saw that grade."

Marc hugged her. "I'm glad you're seeing it my way for a change," he teased.

He took a giant bite of the carrot he'd packed in his lunch that morning. As he crunched on it, he looked down at the bleachers as if he were thinking.

"You know what, Dee?" he said finally. "I've probably been blowing everything out of proportion anyway. You haven't been that distracted. I guess I just needed you with me more, that's all. And it was my birthday. I was just feeling sorry for myself."

"I want to be with you all the time," Dee said. "I know I've been neglecting you a little." She took another sip of juice. "I was so excited about this weekend I even forgot to ask how your grandmother's doing."

"She's better. Mom said the doctor's letting her go home tomorrow."

"Great!"

"Want to go visit her with me tonight?"

"Sure." Dee beamed at him.

But her smile didn't last long because Marc leaned over and kissed her gently on the lips.

"Do you realize where we are?" he asked.

"You mean at the soccer field?"

"No. I mean we're sitting right above where I found you that day last fall. You know — you were watching the team practice. I came up behind you. I first told you I loved you right down there."

Marc pointed through the bleachers to the ground below. "My feelings sure haven't changed," he said.

"Neither have mine," Dee said.

Without another word, Marc took her in his arms and held her tightly for a moment. Then his lips found hers again, this time more hungrily.

"What a way to have lunch," Marc whispered.

Chapter
17

"We have so little time to work this out," Amy said. A worried frown wrinkled her forehead. "What are we going to say?"

Amy held Colin's hand tightly for reassurance as they sat together on the very same bench where he'd kissed her for the first time just three days before. She stared down at the river. Instead of looking beautiful as it had Friday afternoon, the water was rough. The waves seemed to Amy to be about as agitated as she felt inside, especially since she knew she had to confront Susan in only a few more minutes.

"We'll just tell her we like each other," Colin said simply, "and we're thinking of spending every single moment together."

"That sounds so easy!" Amy giggled.

"It is! Susan can't do anything to hurt you," he assured her.

"But that's not the point." Amy grew serious

again. "I'm worried about hurting *her*. You're all that's made her happy in months. Can't you see how terrible I feel for taking you away from her?"

"Sure, I can see that." Colin smoothed her hair back from her forehead. "But Susan never had me in the first place. You haven't taken me away from anyone."

Amy nodded. What Colin said made sense. Amy knew she couldn't spend the rest of her life hiding out at her father's to avoid her sister. He'd driven her to school today from his apartment, so she hadn't even spoken to Susan since first thing Sunday morning.

"We shouldn't make too big a deal out of talking to her," Colin said. "Anyway, this happens all the time."

"What do you mean?"

"That people can't always get exactly what they want." Colin rubbed his hand over Amy's arm and left a path of warmth on her skin. "Don't worry, Amy. Susan'll find somebody else. In another few weeks she'll be talking about some other guy who's more right for her than I am."

"I don't know," Amy said softly. "She's never been so excited about anybody."

Colin smiled. "I guess I should be flattered. But I wish this weren't happening."

"Me, too." Amy sighed. If Colin only knew how much she wished it weren't happening. Having him there when she talked to Susan would help a lot. His support meant everything. But Amy still hated what she had to face. There was no getting around it.

"So, are you ready?" Colin asked.

161

Amy frowned. "I won't ever be."

"Well, then, can you force yourself up from this bench and go with me to your house?" Colin grinned at her.

"Okay. If you put it that way."

Colin hugged her for a minute. Then he bent down and kissed her lightly on the lips. Amy would have given anything to sit right there with him for the rest of the afternoon.

On any other day, riding along the street toward her house with Colin would have been a joy. But today Amy pedaled along with as much enthusiasm as if she were really going to the dentist. When they finally got to her house, she still felt as unprepared for what she had to do as she'd felt all weekend.

And it bothered her how much she wished she could avoid her own sister. She and Susan may have had fights once in a while over the years, but they'd always been close, especially since their parents' problems started. To risk hurting that closeness was what really bothered Amy most as she and Colin started down the sidewalk toward her front door.

"Don't worry, Amy. We'll take care of this just fine," Colin said. He reached for her hand to give it an encouraging squeeze.

Just at that moment, Amy glanced up at the living room window and saw Susan looking outside straight at her and Colin. Susan's mouth dropped open in surprise. As their eyes met, Amy's stomach tied itself into a double knot. She watched as Susan slowly turned her head away from the window as if nothing had happened.

At that moment Amy knew there was no turning back. Susan had seen Colin holding her hand. She and Colin hadn't even had a chance to explain yet, and Susan already knew.

This whole confrontation was starting out even worse than Amy had imagined. Part of her wished she could run away but she knew she couldn't do anything but face her sister.

Amy opened the front door slowly. When she and Colin walked into the living room, they found Susan lying on the sofa, her algebra book open on her stomach and Sam at her feet. She lifted her head to greet them.

Amy was puzzled by the bland, unreadable expression on Susan's face. She'd expected her sister to be angry or in tears, but Susan's eyes met hers without such strong emotions. If Amy hadn't known it couldn't be possible, she'd have thought Susan even looked happy.

"Ready to start?" Susan asked Colin, as if today were no different from their last tutoring session.

"Sure, in a minute," Colin said and smiled. He and Amy sat down in two chairs across from Susan. Colin crossed his ankle over his knee and leaned forward, holding onto the toe of his loafer. "We need to talk to you for a minute first, though," he said, after clearing his throat awkwardly.

"What about?" Susan asked and looked straight at Amy.

Amy flinched. Susan wasn't making it easy for her. Amy looked at Colin. For her life she couldn't have choked out a single word.

"Amy and I really like each other," Colin began. "And — "

"Don't bother explaining, Colin," Susan interrupted. Her mouth turned up into an impish grin. "I just saw you outside."

"How can you be smiling?" Amy asked in amazement.

"Because I want to," Susan replied with a carefree shrug.

"You mean you're not upset?" Amy narrowed her eyes, mystified.

"I know I should be," Susan said lightly. "It's not every day your own sister steals your crush!"

Amy stared at her in disbelief. Susan couldn't be acting so happy after what Colin had just said. Not after she'd been talking about nothing but him all week.

"What's going on, Susan?" Amy exclaimed, her curiosity getting the better of her.

"Nothing," Susan said. Her blue eyes sparkled innocently. "I just don't want to hold a grudge against my own sister."

"But you're supposed to be angry," Amy said.

Susan lay her head back against the sofa pillows and giggled. "Hey, Colin," she said mischievously. "You sure do have a great brother."

"You met Rich?" Colin asked, looking as confused as Amy.

"Uh-huh. We played tennis yesterday."

"Did you two get along?" Amy asked, a light dawning on her.

"We had a blast," Susan said. "We're going out next weekend!"

Colin looked over at Amy and grinned. She was so relieved she almost fell off her chair.

"I can't believe it!" she said, shaking her head as she reached for Colin's hand.

"I'll tell you something else you won't believe!" Susan jumped up from the sofa, picked her backpack off the floor and started rummaging through it. She pulled out a sheet of notebook paper. "Look at this," she said, beaming at them. "I got an A-minus on my algebra test!"

"Susan, that's great!" Amy said happily. She jumped up, too, and gave her sister a big hug.

"I knew you could do it." Colin leaned forward and pulled her ponytail lightly.

"I've got this brilliant tutor," Susan said, teasing again. Her eyes went to Colin's. "If you ever need anybody to help you with *your* math, I'll give you his phone number."

Colin tipped his head back and laughed heartily. "Why don't we double on Saturday and celebrate your grade?" he asked.

"Great idea," Susan said. She handed Colin her test. "Look at the A-minus for yourself."

Just then the phone rang, and Susan raced into the kitchen to answer it. Sam leaped down and chased her.

Amy sank down on the sofa where Susan had been. Colin came over to sit beside her. From Susan's conversation in the kitchen, they could tell Rich was on the phone. She was telling him all about Amy and Colin.

"All our worrying was for nothing," Colin said, putting his arm around Amy.

"For sure," Amy agreed. She rested her head against his shoulder. "I still can't believe it."

She looked up at Colin and saw that his eyes had grown serious. She pulled back to ask him what was wrong, but before she had a chance to say anything, he kissed her lightly on the cheek.

"What would you have done if Susan hadn't met Rich?" he asked, his voice quiet. "We'd still be a couple, wouldn't we?"

A tingle ran through her. Colin had called them a "couple." She couldn't think of any more wonderful word.

"It would have been terrible with Susan," she admitted. "But I never could have said no to you."

Colin cupped her face in his hands and bent down to kiss her softly again. The minute his lips warmed hers, Amy knew that everything would be all right now — with Colin *and* with Susan. She couldn't have asked for anything more. She and Colin were together and they were falling in love. She'd been waiting all her life for something this good to happen. And it finally had.

Coming soon. . .
Couples #22
Slow Dancing

Emily would rather have sat this one out, but Ben was already moving to the music. She let him pull her onto the dance floor, where he immediately started stomping and twisting his body around. Just when she thought she might collapse, the lights in the ballroom dimmed, and the band went into a slow dreamy number.

"May I?"

Emily turned around to see Scott holding out his hand, and a tiny gasp of surprise escaped her lips. Her instinct was to stay away from him, but like a magnet she found herself drawn into his outstretched arms. She couldn't fight it, and sliding her hands around his waist, she leaned her head on his shoulder. For a moment they simply stood there, holding each other, and letting the soft music surround them. It was wonderful to be in Scott's arms again.

"You look very elegant in a tuxedo," Emily said.

Her arms shifted a little around Scott's waist, and he smiled down at her with his blue-gray eyes. "You look pretty special yourself."

He let his cheek rest against her hair as he led her in graceful, light turns around the floor. Scott's arms were around her now, and her love for him welled up inside, filling her heart to the breaking point.

"Are you having a good time?" He pulled back a little to look at her.

Emily nodded. "Are you?"

"Right now I am." He gathered her closer again and they went on swaying and holding each other.

They're talented.... They're winners....

CHEERLEADERS®

They're the hottest squad in town!

Don't miss any of these exciting CHEERLEADERS® books!
Order today!   **$2.25 U.S./$2.95 CAN.**

- ☐ 33402-6 #1 **TRYING OUT** Caroline B. Cooney
- ☐ 33403-4 #2 **GETTING EVEN** Christopher Pike
- ☐ 33404-2 #3 **RUMORS** Caroline B. Cooney
- ☐ 33405-0 #4 **FEUDING** Lisa Norby
- ☐ 33406-9 #5 **ALL THE WAY** Caroline B. Cooney
- ☐ 33407-7 #6 **SPLITTING** Jennifer Sarasin
- ☐ 33687-8 #7 **FLIRTING** Diane Hoh
- ☐ 33689-4 #8 **FORGETTING** Lisa Norby
- ☐ 33705-X #9 **PLAYING GAMES** Jody Sorenson Theis
- ☐ 33815-3 #10 **BETRAYED** Diane Hoh
- ☐ 33816-1 #11 **CHEATING** Jennifer Sarasin
- ☐ 33928-1 #12 **STAYING TOGETHER** Diane Hoh
- ☐ 33929-X #13 **HURTING** Lisa Norby
- ☐ 33930-3 #14 **LIVING IT UP** Jennifer Sarasin
- ☐ 40047-9 #15 **WAITING** Jody Sorenson Theis
- ☐ 40048-7 #16 **IN LOVE** Carol Stanley
- ☐ 40187-4 #17 **TAKING RISKS** Anne Reynolds
- ☐ 40188-2 #18 **LOOKING GOOD** Carol Ellis
- ☐ 37816-3   **CHEERLEADERS BOXED SET**
                   Four Titles: #1 Trying Out, #2 Getting Even, #3 Rumors
                   and #4 Feuding (Not available in Canada)   **$9.00**
- ☐ 40189-0 #19 **MAKING IT** Susan Blake
- ☐ 40190-4 #20 **STARTING OVER** Super Edition Patricia Aks and Lisa Norby
                                         $2.50 U.S./$3.50 CAN.

Scholastic Inc.
P.O. Box 7502, East McCarty Street, Jefferson City, MO 65102

Please send me the books I have checked above. I am enclosing $_____
(please add $1.00 to cover shipping and handling). Send check or money order--no cash or
C.O.D.'s please.

Name_____

Address_____

City_____ State/Zip_____

Please allow four to six weeks for delivery. Offer good in U.S.A. only. Sorry, mail order not available
to residents of Canada.

CHE662